"Let me show you what a Magus can do against a Knight!"

"Nether Resonance!"

Thanatos

SKELETON
KNIGHT IN
ANOTHER WORLD
VIII

written by Ennki Hakari
illustrated by KeG

"Look at this face! Does this seem real to you, hmm?"

> "Even if this world is a game, that doesn't mean you can just do whatever you like!"

Arc

Goemon

"*Today marks the beginning of a new era.*"

Fangas

Sekt

SKELETON KNIGHT IN ANOTHER WORLD

VIII

written by
Ennki Hakari

illustrated by
KeG

Seven Seas

Seven Seas Entertainment

SKELETON KNIGHT IN ANOTHER WORLD VOL. 8

© 2018 Ennki Hakari
Illustrations by KeG

First published in Japan in 2018 by OVERLAP Inc., Ltd., Tokyo.
English translation rights arranged with OVERLAP Inc., Ltd., Tokyo.

Seven Seas press and purchase enquiries can be sent to
Marketing Manager Lianne Sentar at press@gomanga.com.
Information regarding the distribution and purchase of
digital editions is available from Digital Manager CK Russell
at digital@gomanga.com.

Follow Seven Seas Entertainment online at
sevenseasentertainment.com.

TRANSLATION: Jason Muell
ADAPTATION: Peter Adrian Behravesh
COVER DESIGN: Kris Aubin
INTERIOR LAYOUT & DESIGN: Clay Gardner
PROOFREADER: Kris Swanson, Stephanie Cohen
LIGHT NOVEL EDITOR: Nibedita Sen
PREPRESS TECHNICIAN: Rhiannon Rasmussen-Silverstein
PRODUCTION MANAGER: Lissa Pattillo
MANAGING EDITOR: Julie Davis
ASSOCIATE PUBLISHER: Adam Arnold
PUBLISHER: Jason DeAngelis

ISBN: 978-1-64505-977-6
Printed in Canada
First Printing: February 2021
10 9 8 7 6 5 4 3 2 1

SKELETON KNIGHT IN ANOTHER WORLD

VIII

❧ CONTENTS ❧

Rutios Mountains

Central Alsus Cathedral

Fehrbio Alsus

Lione

Holy Hilk Kingdom

Delfrent Kingdom

Iglowa River

Sobir Mountains

Saureah

Morba River

Larisa

Ildbah Forest

Wiel River

Brahniey

Clyde Bay

Ruanne Forest

Fort Hill

Drant

Keen

Salma Kingdom

World Map

Asbania Kingdom

Holy East Revlon Empire

Great West Revlon Empire

Delfrent Kingdom

Great Canada Forest

Salma Kingdom

Rhoden Kingdom

Holy Hilk Kingdom

Nohzan Kingdom

Grand Duchy of Limbult

Map

Prologue

THE SUN BATHED the still field in an amber glow as it slowly set, casting long, dark shadows behind three figures dressed all in black.

At a glance, it was clear these three were cat people, as evidenced by their pointed, feline ears and long, swaying tails. However, the figures were a fair bit larger than the small, lithe forms typically associated with cat people.

The hulking figure leading the group stood at an impressive 2.3 meters tall, and ran through the tall grass at a speed seemingly impossible for his massive build. Even a horse would have struggled to keep up with him, though the other two managed to keep pace.

The three cat people came to a large wheat field, but even the tall stalks didn't slow them. The wheat rustled as if struck by a strong gust of wind, raining leaves and kernels down upon the runners.

They were still a ways off from their objective, but a strange scent in the air caught their attention. Mountain people, after all, were renowned for their superior sense of smell.

"Goemon..."

One of the trailing men called out to their leader, without slowing.

The man up front, Goemon, looked back and nodded.

The air smelled of war—a unique blend of blood, fire, and steel—and stank of death. It had been far too short a time since Goemon had last encountered this scent.

When he'd traveled to the southern continent, he came across the very same mix of smells as thousands of undead soldiers laid waste to the peaceful human settlement of Tagent. The scene had been seared into his mind.

Despite this troubling scent, Goemon pushed on, not slowing his pace until they finally left the wheat field and caught sight of their objective: the capital of the Delfrent Kingdom.

The capital was surrounded by a massive wall to keep out intruders, though it now lay in ruins. The town beyond could be seen through large gaps in the once-strong defenses. Fires raged in the streets, and dark, billowing smoke rose up to blacken the sky.

Goemon drew to a stop so he and his companions could survey the besieged city. Thanks to their superb eyesight, they were able to make out figures moving within.

Though Goemon and his two comrades were some of the most highly trained members of the Jinshin clan, the sheer number of invaders was enough to give them pause.

Goemon spoke in a low, steady voice as he scanned the battlefield. "Quite a few out there."

Hordes of undead soldiers stretched as far as the eye could see, interspersed with the occasional man-spider overseeing the carnage.

There had to be at least 10,000 outside the wall alone.

However, they seemed to be milling about aimlessly, almost sluggishly. Their lack of aggression suggested that the battle was already won, that the capital had fallen. But if that were the case, they almost certainly would have moved on to their next objective. They must be looking for something, then.

The capital itself was quite large, its population plentiful. It would take some time to completely obliterate the city. As for what the undead intended to do with the surviving populace, the obvious answer was that they would add the citizens to their ranks.

This was a horrific fate, no question, though Goemon struggled to summon sympathy for humans, who'd subjugated both his people and the elves at the behest of the Hilk. He didn't take any particular joy in watching their destruction, but neither did he feel sorrow in seeing those who'd burnt down his villages suffer.

Besides, there was no way he and his two companions would be any match for the tens of thousands of undead soldiers lurking about. Even if he'd wanted to help, there was nothing he could do but watch their numbers swell.

"Goemon, look." One of his companions pointed at something off in the distance.

Goemon followed the man's gaze.

On the walkway of the ruined city wall stood a lone figure. Even with their impressive eyesight, the cat people couldn't make out any features, though they could tell that the person was young.

At first, Goemon thought the figure might be a survivor of the carnage below, but they didn't seem particularly troubled by the hordes of undead milling about.

Suddenly, the figure turned and looked straight at them. Goemon scowled back, briefly locking eyes with the diminutive individual before they jumped down off the wall.

"Whaaa?!"

This caught the three cat people completely by surprise. The small figure landed easily on the ground and began rushing straight toward them.

It moved in a fast, jerky manner, almost like a leaping insect. Whatever it was, it clearly wasn't human.

"What is that thing?"

Goemon ignored the question and focused on the approaching figure, trying to figure out how this humanoid creature could move so fast. He turned to his two comrades.

"Return to the rendezvous point as planned!"

The two men nodded, then took off back toward the sea of wheat. They soon vanished from sight.

Goemon glanced at the oncoming creature before taking off in another direction, slipping away into darkness as night fell upon the plains.

The sprawling city of Lione, once the proud capital of the Delfrent Kingdom, had been transformed into a necropolis.

On any normal day, the early evening hours would find the streets full of residents in search of a drink or other worldly pleasures. This merriment had been replaced by the ominous clank of hundreds upon thousands of undead soldiers searching for lingering survivors.

Flames burned bright as the soldiers ravaged once-proud houses, casting an eerie, hellish glow across the city. Bizarre, mutated creatures that looked like a sick amalgamation of human and spider roamed the streets as well.

Fiery pillars of former homes illuminated the large, open squares where the inhabitants had once shared their happiest moments, keeping the encroaching night at bay... for now.

Man-spiders dragged the residents' corpses into one such square and piled them high, creating a literal mountain of bodies. The scene would have roiled even the strongest of stomachs, but the creatures continued their duties, seemingly unfazed.

Even the undead, who'd once been among the corpses that lay before them, moved about with no hesitation, as if they were performing any other menial task. It all would have made for a rather alarming sight, had there been any onlookers.

Dressed in ornate, flowing robes and wielding a holy scepter, an ominous figure with a veil draped over his face knelt in front of the mound of bodies, apparently praying. From a distance, one might easily mistake him for a high-ranking member of the clergy.

However, what the man was actually doing was a far cry from any natural prayer.

The end of the scepter hit the cobblestones with a loud clack. The man raised his right hand into the air, and a stone sitting in his upraised palm began emitting a dark, swirling light.

The glowing stone rose from the holy man's hand and shot soundlessly into the pile of corpses.

The bodies twitched, like ragdolls dumped onto the floor. Soon, they began standing under their own power.

At first glance, it looked as if the man were using magic to perform some kind of resurrection. But upon closer inspection, there was no life to be found in the reanimated residents' eyes, which rolled around without purpose as they all dove into the giant pyre in the middle of the square.

The flames charred their flesh, filling the air with the choking stench of burnt meat.

After allowing their flesh to be completely consumed by flames, the bare skeletons lurched back out of the pyre, leaving trails of charred skin and muscle behind them.

The priestly looking man waved his hand, and the skeletons formed ranks in the square, standing at attention.

"I hate having to recruit my soldiers manually. It's such a hassle."

The holy man let out a sigh and turned his attention to the next mound of bodies.

The man's name was Thanatos Sylvius Hilk, and he was pontiff of the Hilk church, the most influential religion among humans on the northern continent. He was also the one responsible for turning this glorious capital into a city of the dead.

Occasionally, superheated air from the pyre blasted past the pontiff, sending his veil fluttering in the breeze. Had anyone been around, they would have seen nothing but a skull with a flickering red flame where his face should have been.

Thanatos looked around, sensing that someone was near, and fixed his gaze on a young boy emerging from the shadows. He stood out like a sore thumb among all the undead.

Blond-haired and blue-eyed, the stunning young man seemed entirely untroubled by the bizarre scene unfolding around him. He walked straight toward the pontiff and took a knee.

"Apologies, Your Holiness." A high-pitched voice betrayed the boy's young age. "I spotted what appeared to be three beastmen outside the city walls, but I'm afraid that I wasn't able to catch any of them."

Thanatos nodded and gave a dismissive wave of his hand. "Worry not, Tismo. The Delfrent Kingdom has no relationship with the beastmen. There is little concern that they would utter a word to other humans about what happened here."

The pontiff let out a laugh that reverberated in his hollow skull.

After all, it was on the Holy Hilk Kingdom's orders that its neighboring kingdoms had expelled all elves and beast people from their lands over the past few decades.

These non-human creatures had the ability to sense when the undead were present. They posed a threat to the pontiff's plans, so he'd taken it upon himself to drive them out of the surrounding regions once he'd taken his place as ruler.

He'd pursued them to their hidden settlements in the mountains and burned everything to the ground, using their bodies to swell the ranks of his undead armies.

After securing a large enough force, he'd begun collecting rune stones. It was then a simple matter to manufacture the weaponry needed to arm his soldiers.

His forces now numbered in the millions.

It had taken a great deal to get this far, but it had all been worth it. Now was the time for his armies to shine.

The young man standing before Thanatos was Tismo Ghoula Temprantia, the youngest and most powerful of the pontiff's seven cardinals.

"I need to focus on creating as many additional soldiers as I can. I want you to stay on alert. If you see any signs of trouble, handle it. This task will take some time to complete."

"Understood."

Cardinal Tismo bowed low in acknowledgement before leaving the courtyard with several man-spiders in tow.

Thanatos's jaw clacked in another ominous laugh.

"The real game is finally about to begin."

He turned his attention back to the task of creating more undead soldiers.

SKELETON
KNIGHT IN
ANOTHER WORLD

CHAPTER 1

The Alliance

I SQUINTED MY EYES as I gazed up at the bright blue sky.

The ground beneath me shook with the roar of the crowd, the reverberations traveling through the earth and up into my body. I lay on my back, squinting against the brilliant sun.

I was deep in the Great Canada Forest, in the elven capital city of Maple, a place where no human had ever set foot. The massive stadium in the center of the city was filled with excited spectators who'd come to see the event up close.

From the outside, the stadium reminded me of the massive Roman Colosseum. But unlike its real-world counterpart, this one was constructed of massive wooden pillars reinforced with stone, giving it a rather unique look.

There were limited seats, but these were all filled with elves.

The majority of the stadium was devoted to the event space itself, suggesting that it hadn't been built with spectator sports in mind.

Today's entertainment? That was for me to decide.

I turned my gaze away from the blinding sun and back toward the two-meter-tall woman standing next to me. She was smiling from ear to ear.

This was no normal woman. Long, violet hair rustled in the wind around two large horns that shot straight into the sky. Her violet, lizard-like eyes focused on me. Two small wings flapped at her back.

She had a pale body with an hourglass figure and a large chest—which was where many people's eyes went first. Most notable, however, were the dark scales that ran from her shoulders to her arms and down her back, like natural armor.

A similarly scaled tail, almost as long as she was tall, jutted from her lower back, its tip covered in jagged crystals.

This was Felfi Visrotte, one of the Dragon Lords.

She was at the top of the figurative food chain in this world. Though her true form was that of a dragon, she was also able to look humanoid. Even in this relatively diminutive body, however, she was still able to bring her full power to bear.

Her immense power would undoubtedly be a great asset in the upcoming battle against the Holy Hilk Kingdom.

Though she'd referred to this as a game, I suspected her goal was to show off just how powerful she was to all the elves who gathered to watch.

She'd won in the end, and left me lying in a heap of gleaming armor on the stadium floor, but I still managed to put up a good fight. At the very least, she seemed satisfied.

I rubbed my throbbing nose and slowly returned to my feet, then picked up my helmet and slid it back over my head, watching out for my dark, elongated ears.

This mock battle had been quite a beneficial experience. It had given me an opportunity to practice keeping my emotions under control in my elven form, an experience I wasn't at all used to after so much time spent in my emotionally stunted skeleton form. It was still too easy for fear to overwhelm me on the field of battle.

All the training I'd undergone recently had definitely helped keep my wits about me against the Dragon Lord. I finally felt as if I were getting used to life here in this world, though whether that was a good or bad thing, I still couldn't say.

I turned my attention back to Felfi Visrotte. She flashed an encouraging grin as she approached me, giving me a once-over before her gaze settled on the Holy Thunder Sword of Caladbolg.

"That last blow was a good one. But you were still holdin' back, weren't ya?" Her reptilian eyes narrowed, like a hunter sizing up its prey.

I shrugged. "I could say the same about you. Unless I'm mistaken, you seemed to be going easy on me too."

She ran a hand through her long, lustrous hair. "If I'd really given it a go, this whole building would be in ruins right now. But that's true for you, too, isn't it? It's not like we could just ignore all the spectators gathered here. At least we had a chance to show your face off to everyone."

Apparently, that had also been one of her goals with this little game. Though, frankly, I was still convinced that the major reason we were here was because she loved a good fight. That's how it had felt in the heat of things.

I recalled the conversation we'd had back at the meeting of the high elders, the group who controlled everything that happened here in Maple. That's where this had all begun.

While I was now a member of Lalatoya Village, I was still a newcomer. No one, least of all the elven soldiers, was too keen on me being a lynchpin in the upcoming battle. Even if the execution was a bit ham-fisted for my liking, I had a feeling that this had also been an opportunity to show off my skills against a powerful Dragon Lord, to mitigate further misgivings.

Out of the corner of my eye, I saw a lithe, well-proportioned figure wearing a robe marked with intricately detailed runes make her way down from the spectator seats and approach us.

The woman had golden eyes, amethyst skin, and pointed ears that poked out of her long, snow-white hair. She was a dark elf, which was somewhat rare in this world.

Her name was Ariane, and she was not only from the same village as me, but also one of my closest friends since I'd first arrived in this world.

She looked at the woman next to me with great concern. "Felfi Visrotte, are you all right?"

Ariane's golden gaze darted between the Dragon Lord's stomach and her face. She was clearly concerned about when I'd stabbed her during the battle. However, Felfi Visrotte simply slid her hand along the ribbed scales of her stomach and laughed.

"There's nothing to worry about here. It takes a lot more than that to actually hurt me."

Ariane let out a sigh of relief. "I... Wow. I see." She lowered her voice and whispered to me. "I dunno, Arc, that looked like a fatal blow from where we were sitting. What happened?"

All I could do was shrug. "I'm also at a loss. I felt the blade go in, so it wasn't just some illusion, but I still can't figure it out. The best I can say is that there's something special about the Dragon Lord's humanoid form."

Ariane turned back to find Felfi Visrotte waving enthusiastically at the spectators.

A little furry animal dove toward us from the stands, its green fur rippling in the wind.

Standing at about sixty centimeters—half of which was its long, cotton-like tail—Ponta had the face of a fox, and thin membranes that ran between its front and hind legs, allowing it to glide through the air.

"Kyii! Kyiiiii!"

This adorable creature mewing for attention was what the elves called a spirit creature. After a quick flip in the air, it landed atop my helmet.

"Hey, Ponta, what's up?"

It seemed to be offering its encouragement about the battle. I reached up and scratched the top of its head.

"Kyii!"

Ponta batted its front paws against the side of my helmet, directing my attention back toward the stands. I noticed a figure waving me over.

"It looks like we're being summoned, Ariane."

Ariane turned as well and nodded in acknowledge-ment. "I'm afraid we must be going now, Felfi Visrotte."

The Dragon Lord finished waving at the crowd and smiled at us. "No problem, I had a great time today. I'll play my part later, just like I promised. Oh, and Arc, let's play again sometime, eh?"

There was something about the smile on her face that sent a chill up my spine. "Ah, umm, yes. We'll see if an opportunity presents itself..."

With that, Ariane and I—with Ponta sitting proudly atop my head—headed back to the spectators' seats. Before we'd made it halfway, Felfi Visrotte called out to me.

"Oh, one more thing! I wanted to ask you to pass along a message for me, Arc."

Glancing back, I saw the Dragon Lord regarding me with a slight scowl.

"A message for whom?" I couldn't think of anyone we both knew who wasn't currently in the stadium.

Her expression softened, and she waved her hand dis-missively. "You know what? Don't you worry your pretty little head about it. It'll be faster if I do it myself anyway. See ya later, Arc!"

The small wings on her back began flapping vigorously, and a moment later, she disappeared into the sky.

Her parting words had left a bad taste in my mouth. I really hoped to avoid facing against her again. But judging by the cheerful expression on her face, it seemed unlikely I'd be able to put her off forever, especially while I was living here among the elves.

I let out a heavy sigh.

"Kyii?" Ponta looked down curiously at me, so I reached up to scratch its chin.

"It's nothing, Ponta."

The high elders in the stands who'd come to watch the event were staring at me with great interest. Apparently, the elves were shocked to see someone face off against a Dragon Lord and live to tell the tale. Or at least, that was what I took from the looks of surprise, and suspicion, on their faces.

However, there was one person who stood out from the rest of the elders: the third founder, Briahn Bond Evanjulin Maple, head of the high elders and ruler of the entire Great Canada Forest.

Ribbons of all shapes and colors adorned his green-tinted blond hair, and elegant necklaces hung low around his neck, indicating his incredibly high status.

When he finally spoke, the surprise in his voice was unmistakable. "Well, I certainly wouldn't believe what just happened if I hadn't seen it with my own two eyes. I have to admit, when Dillan told me that there was someone who could stand toe-to-toe with the great Dragon Lord Felfi Visrotte, I was skeptical. But if you truly are this powerful, I can't see how anyone would object to you leading our elven forces."

Fangas Flan Maple—another dark elf, who was one of the high elders and Ariane's maternal grandfather—nodded in agreement.

He was about my height, but his body was absolutely immense and covered in muscles. His short-cropped white hair, the large scar running along his face, and his well-trimmed beard all contributed to his intimidating appearance. He looked like he'd be much more at home on the battlefield. However, he seemed to be in good spirits right now.

"I haven't seen a fight that impressive in quite a while! I hope you'll let me spar with you sometime."

He grinned broadly and clapped his heavy hands down on my shoulders. The forceful act caused Ponta to cry out in annoyance.

"Kyii! Kyiiiii!"

It looked like I'd be pretty busy sparring once this battle was out of the way.

I'd always figured the elves to be a mostly magical people, though I'd recently started realizing that sheer physical strength might win the day here. In retrospect, this was hardly surprising. Surrounded on all sides by powerful monsters and dangerous humans, strength was all the elves had to fall back on.

I averted my gaze in an attempt to avoid responding to Fangas's offer, only to spot two more figures approaching: village elder Dillan Tahg Lalatoya and Eevin Glenys Maple, Ariane's father and sister, respectively.

Unlike Ariane, Dillan had the characteristic green-tinted blond hair of most elves. He was dressed in priestly robes covered in intricate runes. He looked exactly like my mental image of an elf, especially when compared to the battle-hungry high elder Fangas.

He bowed his head slightly. "Good job, Arc. It'll be a bit of a rush, but we should be able to muster our soldiers for battle in about a day. You can take the rest of today off to relax and prepare for tomorrow. We'll be relying on you to teleport everyone, after all."

I glanced over at Ariane, who tilted her head curiously.

"If it's all right with you, I'd like to spend the rest of the day touring your great capital."

There wasn't really much for me to do when it came to mustering the troops, so I figured now was my chance to look around Maple, the capital city of the Great Canada Forest.

Sure, now that I'd been here once I'd be able to use Transport Gate to teleport here whenever I wanted, but it felt like such a waste not to do some sightseeing on my very first visit.

Dillan glanced at Briahn, who smiled softly and nodded. "Of course. I'm sure Ariane would be more than happy to show you around. However, don't forget that we still need to tell the humans that we've agreed to offer our assistance."

Dillan clapped his hands together, eliciting a heavy sigh from Ariane.

"All right, but we can't be out too long, okay? Don't forget that Chiyome and Riel are both waiting on us."

I nodded. I wanted to take my time looking around the city, but Princess Riel and the others were probably anxiously awaiting our response.

Before I could dwell on this further, a newcomer butted into the conversation.

"If my darling little Arin is going, then I'm going too!" Eevin, Ariane's older sister, clung tightly to Ariane's arm and raised a fist in her father's direction before he could put up an argument.

A dark elf, like her younger sister, Eevin wore her white hair short, down to her shoulders. She was also a lot more energetic than her cooler-headed sibling.

Ariane could barely contain her surprise. "Why're you coming along, Eevin?!"

Eevin puffed out her cheeks in anger.

Ariane quickly backpedaled, waving her hand as if to brush the whole issue away. "I-I mean...you're coming too? Don't you have a lot of work to do to prepare for tomorrow, Sis?"

Ariane seemed to stumble over the word "Sis," glancing at me in embarrassment. It seemed she only used this endearment behind closed doors.

I felt Eevin's eyes on me, growing more and more intense as she clung to Ariane's arm. She didn't seem too keen on me coming between her and her little sister.

She turned her attention back to Ariane. "It's just a little excursion, y'know. I figure I can bring along my usual gear. Don't worry, I've got tons of time! Besides, don't you want to see your big sis in her element?"

Dillan interrupted his daughter for a slight correction. "Unfortunately, you won't be coming with us on this journey, Eevin."

She wasn't pleased with this. "What?! Whyyyy? This is one of Canada's greatest battles, isn't it? You'll need fighters like me! What's going on here?"

Dillan shook his head and let Fangas explain instead.

"That's precisely why you can't go, Eevin. If all of our

greatest soldiers leave the capital, Maple will be un-defended. I'm entrusting the capital's guards to you while I'm away...which also means that I'll be joining the fight. Gyahaha!"

"Whoa, whoa... That's not fair, Grandpa! What's a high elder doing going into battle?! If that's not an abuse of power, I don't know what is!"

Fangas let out a hearty laugh. "If it's such a big deal, then you best rise through the ranks, Eevin."

She clenched her jaw. This didn't seem to bother Fangas one bit.

The high elders oversaw the operation of every village within the Great Canada Forest, and thus rarely ventured out on military excursions. However, it was evident from Fangas's hulking figure that he prided himself on his martial skills.

Judging from what Eevin had said, Fangas had used his influence in order to secure himself a place on the front line.

Dillan and Briahn smiled as they watched the two argue. This confrontation clearly wasn't unexpected.

I whispered to Ariane. "So, why are we still standing here listening? Does the outcome matter to us?"

"Kyii?" Ponta mewed in curiosity.

Ariane let out a sigh. "Come on. Let's give you a tour."

Most elves lived in the Great Canada Forest here on the northern continent. Monsters roamed these woods, but they also served as an additional layer of protection against the humans.

I have to admit, I was pretty surprised to learn that this land had once been nothing but empty plains. Then the founding elder had come along and created an artificial forest and, hidden deep in the inner reaches, the capital of Maple, a city so advanced that it defied human imagination. It was absolutely nothing like anything else I'd seen in this world.

The city was filled with tree buildings that shot into the sky, an intriguing amalgamation of nature and technology. Elves went about their lives up on the elevated, open-air walkways that stretched between the buildings.

The streets were perfectly laid out and lined with lights at regular intervals, providing more than ample illumination for the customers milling about the shops and the tradespeople practicing their crafts.

As I watched the large crowd bustle through the valleys between the trees, I felt something nagging at the back of my mind.

It hadn't been all that long since I'd first come to this world. And yet, as I finally accepted that I'd likely never return to my home, I felt sorrow wash over me.

In addition to the founding elder of the Great Canada Forest, there was also Hanzo, the man who'd saved the cat people from persecution and formed the Jinshin clan, before making his way to the southern continent to create a kingdom for the mountain people down there. They were both almost certainly wanderers brought to this world like myself.

I wondered if they ever missed the world they came from. Alas, it wasn't like anyone alive now would know anything about that. They'd both died, as far as I knew.

Dwelling on it wouldn't do me any good.

Fortunately, I didn't have to worry about troublesome emotions while I was in my skeleton form. I could just continue on my merry way, with little concern for things like this.

There was, however, a downside. As soon as I drank from the mystical spring near the Lord Crown to lift my curse, not only did I return to my elven form, but all the pent-up emotions came flooding back as well.

Once this battle was over, I'd probably need to have a good, long think about getting myself used to dealing with emotions again.

As well as spending the rest of my life here, for that matter.

Ariane glanced over her shoulder, puzzled. "What's with you, Arc? You were the one who said you wanted to look around, but you haven't said anything about what you wanted to see. The city's pretty big, y'know. It'd take a few days just to see everything."

"Kyii! Kyiiiii!"

Ponta mewed in agreement.

I decided to banish the dark thoughts from my mind for now. "Ah, sorry, Ariane. I was just thinking about what I wanted to see before our time runs out. I think I'd like to visit a store that sells magical elven items. Do you know a good place?"

"Magical items? Hmm, I guess I know a few places."

While Ariane stopped to think, Eevin finally broke her long silence and chimed in. "Well, why don't we go to the place Arin and I usually buy our stuff from?"

Ariane nodded and smiled. "Oh, right! The place we always go to! Sounds good."

With that, Ariane began leading the way through the crowded streets. I drew curious looks, as usual. I tried to shrug them off, yet I couldn't help but sense someone paying a little too much attention to me.

Looking over, I caught sight of Eevin staring intensely at me.

"Kyii?" Ponta let out a confused yelp at Eevin's sudden change in demeanor.

"Have I done something wrong?"

Eevin averted her gaze and took a few steps away from me to put more distance between us. Before I could say anything more, however, she beat me to the punch.

Her voice was cold. "So…I know you can hold your own in battle. I saw that much back in the stadium. But I want you to know that if anything happens to my darling little Arin, I'll make sure you regret it."

She pointed right at me to punctuate her words. I was too intimidated to reply. It was all I could do to nod dumbly in response.

"Yes, ma'am. I mean, Miss Eevin. I promise that I will protect Ariane with my life."

The upcoming battle was going to be an intense one, probably the most dangerous thing we'd faced yet. It was easy to understand why she'd be worried about her little sister, especially since she couldn't come with us.

Deep down, I knew it was just a tad arrogant for me to say that I would protect Ariane, especially considering how strong a fighter she was in her own right. But now

hardly seemed like the time or place to bring up such trivialities.

After all, protecting Ariane had always been Eevin's job. Since she'd admitted that I was a talented fighter in my own right, it only seemed fair for me to take this duty from her.

One way or another, I had to convince her that I would be true. "I promise, I will protect her with my very life."

Eevin raised a thin eyebrow at my cocky reply. "You'd better keep your word."

Having sufficiently drilled the point home, Eevin took off in a jog after Ariane.

There'd be no slacking off for me in the upcoming battle.

With a renewed sense of purpose, I followed the two sisters through the crowds and down a much quieter side street lined with shops.

The building we stopped in front of wasn't marked with any sort of sign, and, quite frankly, I wasn't even sure if it *was* a shop. However, Ariane opened the wooden door, which responded with a loud creak, and walked right in. Eevin, Ponta, and I entered after her.

The interior was dimly lit, and filled to the brim with all sorts of small items, which made it difficult to even move around. Despite this, it still looked quite clean and well taken care of.

One of the walls was lined with shelves from floor to ceiling, every available space filled with equipment. I could even guess what most of them were used for.

I felt like I was in a museum.

Some of the goods looked familiar, so I felt confident enough to guess that these were all magical items of one sort or another.

In the center of the room stood several waist-high shelves displaying unique wares. I felt like I could spend a whole day here and never grow bored.

I mumbled quietly to myself as I cast my gaze across the store. Looking up and toward the back, I caught sight of a small area that seemed like a workshop of sorts.

A moment later, an old man sporting white hair and a white beard that fell to his waist emerged from the workshop area.

He stood at around 140 centimeters, maybe even shorter, and had a thick, barrel-shaped body that made his muscular arms and legs look like afterthoughts that had just been pinned onto him.

Deep wrinkles chiseled into the man's forehead, giving him the intense look of a man who'd lived a long life mastering his craft.

"A dwarf?" The words left my mouth before I had a chance to think better of them.

The old man angled his head to look up at me.

Though they'd once been common across the entire northern continent, the dwarves had been hunted by humans to near extinction. The elves had offered them sanctuary in the Great Canada Forest, letting the humans believe that all the dwarves had died out.

Since coming to Maple, I'd seen quite a few wandering the streets. In fact, one of the high elders was a dwarf.

"Well, I'll be! It's been awhile since I've seen you ladies around these parts. Who's the flashy knight you've got with you?"

The dwarf—store owner and craftsman, as far as I could tell—raised a large, bushy eyebrow at me, with a certain degree of suspicion.

I stepped forward to introduce myself. "I am Arc Lalatoya. I've only recently been invited to join Ariane's village."

"Kyii! Kyiiiii!" Ponta chimed in as well, ending with an exaggerated wag of its tail.

"That's not a cottontail fox, is it? Never seen one sit so easily atop someone's head. You an elf?" The old man gave me a quizzical look.

Ariane stepped in to smooth over the situation.

"You could say that."

Strictly speaking, my non-skeletal form didn't look

anything like the elves or even dark elves that inhabited this world, but her answer was technically correct.

The dwarven man cocked his head at this odd reply, but didn't seem to care enough to push the issue. He turned his attention back to me. "Well, enough about that. What brings y'all here?"

Eevin and Ariane both turned to look at me.

"Now that you mention it, what *did* you come here to buy anyway?"

I reached out to a nearby shelf, picked up the closest item, and brought it to my face for closer inspection. "Well, uh, I just figured that, when this is all over, I'd like to get my shrine into livable condition. There are so many conveniences out here, and I thought this was a good chance to check some of them out."

Ariane, apparently sold on my explanation, turned her attention back to the many wares that lined the shop's shelves. "Now that you mention it, there really isn't much there, other than the hot spring."

"Personally, I'd love to get my hands on something like that magical cooking apparatus that Glenys is always using in the kitchen."

Ariane moved about the shop and picked out several items for me.

Of course, there were the remains of a hearth back in

the shrine, but if I could avoid the hassle of cooking over a wood-fueled fire by purchasing some magical items, then all the better.

Ariane put a finger to her chin in thought, as if recalling what the shrine looked like. "It's pretty dark there at night, too, right? There aren't any lights or anything, so maybe some large crystal lamps would help."

Now that she mentioned it, there were no artificial light sources there at all, leaving me to navigate by the light of the moon at night. Making matters worse, the canopy of the massive Lord Crown blocked much of the sky, plunging the shrine even further into darkness.

While Ariane and I browsed the shop, the owner let out a loud yawn and scratched the top of his head. He spoke in a slow, bored tone. "I dunno. Y'all sound like a newlywed couple buying yer first furniture together."

Ariane's ears burned bright red.

"Whoa, wait a minute! I'm just here to help him shop! Besides, I think Big Sis here is the one who you should be talking to about newlyweds!" Ariane's voice rang with annoyance.

Eevin drew close, however, a bright grin on her face. "Aww, Arin, you called me 'Big Sis'!"

This only seemed to annoy Ariane even more. She tried pushing Eevin away.

I had to admit, the two sisters were adorable when they argued.

The old dwarven man and I exchanged glances. Without needing to say anything, I could tell we were thinking the same thing. We both shrugged, and left the sisters to their spat.

I brought an item over to the owner to ask him about it. "Excuse me, sir, could you please tell me what this is?"

He beamed at my obvious interest in his work and took time to politely answer all of my questions. I began growing excited about my future life, letting the yelling match behind me fade into the background.

After discussing various magical items with the dwarven shop owner, and picking out the ones I wanted to bring back to my shrine, I informed him that I would be back later to buy everything. The next time I had a chance to visit, after all, would likely be after the battle with the Holy Hilk Kingdom.

After we left the shop, Eevin said her goodbyes. Ariane, Ponta, and I returned to Lalatoya to tell Chiyome about what had happened at the meeting of the high elders.

The short girl in ninja garb spoke up the moment she caught sight of me. "How did everything work out in Maple?"

Despite her small stature, her clear, azure gaze carried a strength that many adults could never possess.

The cat ears atop her head, and the black tail that extended from her waist, marked her as one of the mountain people. More specifically, she was of the feline variety.

Ariane was the first to respond. "Don't you worry, Chiyome. The central council officially agreed to join the battle."

Chiyome let out a loud breath. "I...see. Well, I suppose it's settled then."

Her face tensed as she asked her next question. "So, do you know how large a force we'll need to completely wipe out the undead army?"

This was probably the most important question of all, since the Holy Hilk Kingdom's forces numbered in the hundreds of thousands.

If we didn't do anything to stop them, humans, mountain people, and elves alike would find themselves in a very dangerous situation. However, a direct frontal assault on an army of that size would only accelerate the grim future that awaited us.

And yet, here we were, with species who'd spent generations doing their best to avoid each other putting aside their grievances to fight a common threat. It was as if fate itself had intervened.

I could tell by the look in Chiyome's eyes that this weighed heavily on her, and that she was committed to our victory.

To the human nations that had lost almost everything, and were hanging on by a thread, this might have looked like a step back. However, it was a necessary step, in order to ensure that this world lived on.

For myself, I couldn't help but wonder if it truly was chance that had brought me here from another world and placed me at the center of such a pivotal battle. In my heart of hearts, I felt that there must have been some sort of supernatural influence involved. I didn't actually expect to learn the answer to this question though, nor would the answer change what I had to do.

Asking God about the purpose of your life was just as useful here as it was back in my world.

In the end, it was up to me to pursue my dreams. Fortunately, I had the abilities to make them reality.

The teleportation magic that allowed be to cross vast distances in the blink of an eye was what had enabled me to bring these three species together in the first place.

The Holy Hilk Kingdom had first attacked its nearest neighbors, but now that they'd been overrun, it was only a matter of time until the undead arrived at the capital of the Nohzan Kingdom.

Fortunately, the elves understood the severity of the situation and had agreed to form an alliance with the humans.

I was worried that the elves would choose to stand by and watch the humans get wiped out, but since that would mean facing an even larger undead army all on their own, it made sense for them to join the battle now.

Which led me to Felfi Visrotte. From my sparring match with the Dragon Lord, I'd learned firsthand that she was immensely powerful.

She and the other three Dragon Lords lived here in the Great Canada Forest and offered their protection to all who dwelt within.

If we could convince them to join us as well, then we could topple the Hilk, despite the fact that most humans were still faithful to the church's teachings.

The high elders knew this, yet had done nothing to rally the other Dragon Lords. The only explanation I could think of was that there was some kind of agreement between the Dragon Lords and the elves, and that Felfi Visrotte was the only one allowed to take a more active role in the affairs of the world.

Even so, this battle—no, this war—against the Holy Hilk Kingdom should be winnable.

"You have nothing to worry about, Chiyome. The people of the Great Canada Forest have made arrangements for a Dragon Lord to assist us in battle. Not only that, but they've agreed to muster a large number of troops as well."

Chiyome's eyes went wide.

Ariane spoke in a soothing voice as she put a reassuring hand on Chiyome's shoulder. "That's right. Not only is Felfi Visrotte said to be the strongest of the Dragon Lords, but we've also got Arc with us, and he's already destroyed over 100,000 undead soldiers on his own."

After having turned Sasuke, Chiyome's brother-in-arms, into a member of the undead, the Holy Hilk Kingdom had become Chiyome's mortal enemy. Ariane and I were all too aware that she would stop at nothing to see them defeated.

It was just as personal for Ariane, who'd been there when Chiyome was forced to kill Sasuke in battle. She knew that if we weren't careful, Chiyome may decide to fight the Holy Hilk Kingdom on her own.

Though she was still a girl, Chiyome was, in fact, one of the greatest warriors of the Jinshin clan. Survival had been drilled into her from a young age. She understood that allying ourselves with the humans was the only way we could achieve victory.

For people like Sasuke and Chiyome, who'd spent their lives killing, learning to separate their hearts from their minds was vital.

I let my thoughts wander, thinking again about the strange sequence of events that had brought me here... and where I would go next. I began explaining my plan.

"Tomorrow, I'll use Transport Gate to teleport all the elven soldiers to the Nohzan capital. Since we don't have much time, I plan to head back to the Rhoden Kingdom and notify Princess Riel and the others waiting there shortly."

"In that case, I'd like to go with you," Chiyome said.

Ariane looked relieved at Chiyome's renewed determination.

"Also, um, would you mind taking me to the Nohzan Kingdom after you're done with that, Arc? I'm not sure which route they took, but Goemon and the others should be arriving any day now."

I was also curious about what they'd encountered on their way to the capital. I didn't say it aloud, but I was worried about our friends' well-beings.

It was a little late to be only thinking about this now, but I also needed to make arrangements in the Nohzan Kingdom to bring in such a large number of troops. Between the Rhoden Kingdom and the Great Canada

Forest, there would be at least 10,000 soldiers joining the fight.

Of course, 10,000 was practically nothing in the face of 100,000 undead, but that was where Felfi Visrotte and I would come in.

"All right. Let's head to the Rhoden Kingdom to speak with Princess Riel."

I hefted my bag, and Ponta let out a yawn. This whole thing was all pretty boring for my little buddy.

"Kyiiii..."

Alas, things would heat up quickly in the next day or so.

I reached up and stroked its fur, then summoned up Transport Gate to take us all to the Rhoden Kingdom.

Early the next morning, while a thin, white mist still gripped the city, a large crowd gathered anxiously in Maple's massive stadium.

These were the soldiers who would be leaving the safety of the Great Canada Forest to join the fight against the Holy Hilk Kingdom.

Most were outfitted in leather armor, with only the occasional flash of metal in between.

More interesting, however, was the sheer variety of weapons, each soldier armed with whatever they were most skilled with. The various bags and belongings they brought also spoke to the diversity of the villages this ragtag group was leaving behind.

There were even a few soldiers with the characteristic amethyst skin of dark elves.

I have to admit that I'd assumed most of the soldiers would be men, but I was surprised to find that at least a third of them were women. This was in stark contrast to the human military, which was heavily male-dominated.

Between Ariane, her mother, Glenys, and her sister, Eevin, I already knew quite a few female soldiers. I wondered if elven culture had harbored a bias against female warriors in the first place, or if they were just quicker to move away from outdated gender roles.

"I guess Ariane and Glenys really weren't exceptions after all, huh?"

"Kyiii..." Ponta responded cheerfully to my quiet musings.

Dillan and Ariane, who'd come along to oversee today's gathering, approached me.

Ariane, for some reason, was glaring daggers. "What was that just now? Are you trying to insult me, Arc?"

I shook my head quickly. "No, of course not! I was just impressed at how talented elven women are."

"Kyii kyii!"

Ariane glared at me for a few more moments, then let out an annoyed sigh. The sudden shaking of my head had nearly thrown poor Ponta off, so I reached up and slid it back onto its perch atop my helmet.

"All elven soldiers spend their lives training with the weapons and magic they're best at. So, unlike with humans, being a soldier isn't just a matter of having certain physical attributes. I suppose you could say you're more like an elf in that respect."

Up until now, I'd felt a divide between myself and the elves here, but put in that light, there was something to be said for how the Paladin class I was using—with its mixture of both the physicality of the Knight class and the arcanity of the Monk class—was actually pretty close to the fighting style that defined elven soldiers.

Ariane's words sparked a renewed sense of excitement within me. I'd always felt a bit sad that the only real connection I shared with the elves in my non-skeleton form was my elongated ears.

Before I could dwell on this further, Dillan approached with Fangas in tow. "Well, Arc, we're counting on you to bring all these soldiers to the Nohzan Kingdom."

Fangas spoke next. "So, I hear you're going to be using teleportation magic. I know enough not to doubt someone that Ariane trusts so implicitly, but I have to wonder if it's truly necessary to teleport everyone at once. If something goes wrong, the battle will be lost before it even begins."

The high elder had a point.

While Transport Gate used a lot less magic than offensive spells, expanding it to an area large enough to encompass all of these people would consume a lot of energy, especially over multiple trips.

However, with my Twilight Cloak, I would be able to regenerate a set amount of magical energy any time I was standing still. So long as I took ample breaks, I was confident I could accomplish this in about half a day's time.

When I'd traveled to the Rhoden Kingdom last night to share the good news of Canada's decision with Princess Riel, I'd also met with King Karlon to tell him of my plans to teleport his army to the Nohzan Kingdom. I'd asked him to hurry up their preparations.

Honestly, I was a little concerned about whether they'd be able to muster their troops in time.

They had the command structure in place, of course, but they also needed a lot of people and resources to make it happen. It would be an incredible challenge to get all of that together in short order.

In that regard, it was easier for the elves to form up on such short notice, since they rarely fought in a large army. Each individual soldier was responsible for supplying everything they needed to fight, including food.

This battle was on a vastly different scale from the duties elven soldiers were used to. They usually moved through the forest in small units, sourcing their own rations and weapons. Patrols often lasted several days while they slayed monsters to keep their villages safe.

Still, other than the scale, and the fact that they were traveling to a human country, this wasn't that different from any other elven patrol.

"You have nothing to worry about, Fangas. Speaking of which, I haven't seen Felfi Visrotte yet this morning. Do you know if she's all right? I was hoping to bring her along first, so she has a chance to meet with the humans."

I'd also stopped by the Nohzan Kingdom last night to tell them to make preparations to receive a large number of soldiers. I'd explained to King Asparuh that an incredibly powerful Dragon Lord would be joining the battle as well.

Fangas and Dillan exchanged a knowing glance. Ariane and I looked back at them, confused.

Dillan shook his head. "Felfi Visrotte said that she was going to fly to the Nohzan Kingdom herself. She may be there already, in fact, assuming she didn't spend too long on her side trip."

This probably meant that she was in her Dragon Lord form, since it was better suited to flying. I was impressed that she even knew where these human countries were located.

This did, however, present one problem. I was confident that the elven soldiers would stand their ground when the Dragon Lord entered the battle, but I could easily imagine shock overtaking the humans if they suddenly saw a dragon descend upon their capital.

Thinking back to when I'd first seen Villiers Fim in his dragon form, I could imagine the fear that might induce.

"Hmm. Perhaps it would be best for us to send an elf to explain things to the Nohzan Kingdom before she arrives."

Fangas gave a firm nod. "You're right. Best we avoid causing a panic. I'll supervise the troop movements while Dillan smooths things over with the humans. Can you bring him to Nohzan with a small contingent?"

"Absolutely."

Dillan summoned a nearby group of soldiers who were already packed and ready to go.

I stepped into the center of the stadium, together with Dillan, Fangas, and the soldiers who would serve as our first contingent.

I had everyone huddle together and pull their gear in close so that I could keep the teleportation rune on the ground small and conserve energy.

Since I needed to be at the center of the rune, the area around me was the most cramped.

"I feel like I'm on a commuter train during rush hour..."

"Kyii!" Ponta cheered me on.

I was incredibly jealous of Ponta's privileged spot atop my head.

My armor protected me from actually feeling the crush of bodies all around me, but there was something about being crammed in the middle of a large group that made me think fondly of the past.

Ariane and Chiyome stood outside the range of the teleportation rune, waving. Apparently, they'd decided to wait until things were less crowded.

"Guess we'd better go before someone gets crushed. Come on, Ponta. Transport Gate!"

"Kyii! Kyiiiii!"

A large, glowing rune appeared on the ground as I summoned up the spell. All of the soldiers around me stared down at their feet, speaking in a mixture of surprise and excitement as they watched this unfold.

I closed my eyes and focused on the corner of the castle in the Nohzan Kingdom where King Asparuh had arranged a space for our forces.

Everything went dark, the voices fell silent, and an instant later, we were in a completely different place.

Gone was the Maple stadium, now replaced with the large courtyard next to the castle in Saureah, the capital of the Nohzan Kingdom.

The elves around me let out gasps of surprise. They began venturing out into the courtyard, giving me some space.

I noticed some guards standing around, probably awaiting our arrival, but even though they'd known we were coming, they still looked shocked.

Fangas began issuing orders. "I'm sure this is all fascinating to you, but we don't have time for lollygagging!"

The soldiers immediately hefted their gear and formed behind Fangas. Since we'd be using this same spot to teleport each group in, we needed to keep it clear.

Also, as a representative of the elves, Fangas had to meet with King Asparuh. This initial contingent would serve as his guard. However, looking over his muscle-bound frame, his sturdy leather armor, his massive war hammer, and the intimidating scar running down his face, I found it hard to imagine this man needed much protection.

Given that this initial group was mostly made up of massively built dark elves, I wondered if the humans would even believe these were the forces from the Great Canada Forest.

King Asparuh Nohzan Saureah soon showed up with his own contingent of royal guards in tow.

The two men exchanged greetings while their guards held back.

"I'd like to thank you, on behalf of my entire country, for overcoming interspecies prejudice and offering us your assistance in our darkest hour. We greatly appreciate it."

The king bowed his head to Fangas. The high elder offered a burly hand in return, and the two men shook.

"If we can finally put an end to the Holy Hilk Kingdom, then it will all be worth it. I'm sure this is a difficult time for your people, especially those who still follow the church, but we're more than happy to join you."

That was the entire reason why Canada had agreed to send soldiers in the first place. They intended to use this opportunity to bring the fight to the Hilk church. The fact that the Nohzan Kingdom had accepted aid under these terms was a sign of their assent.

Even though destroying the power base of the Hilk church would dramatically reduce its influence, there were still many kingdoms founded under Hilk principles. The high elders were well aware that these dark teachings wouldn't vanish overnight.

It remained to be seen what form the Hilk religion would take after the fall of the church, but the Nohzan Kingdom, which had only survived annihilation thanks to a united front with the elves, would be instrumental in combatting the religion's resurgence.

And then there was Rhoden, another influential human kingdom outside the Hilk's direct sphere of influence, which would also be offering its support. They would help spread the anti-church sentiments to their neighbors.

Canada was hoping that the Nohzan Kingdom would keep the Holy Hilk Kingdom in check, and had agreed to help them rebuild after the war, in order to provide a stronger defense against the church.

"We've been driven to the edge, and don't have many options left to us, but despite that, I feel that this decision will ensure a bright future for our country. Together, we will forge a brilliant new world."

King Asparuh held Fangas's gaze and gave his hand another firm shake.

A king willingly joining forces with the mountain people and elves would certainly elicit outrage among the true Hilk believers once they heard the news. The shock would be relatively small among those who'd endured the siege here in the capital, but for those living who hadn't yet experienced the wrath of the Holy Hilk Kingdom, they likely wouldn't let this go so easily.

People, after all, tended to hate change. Many didn't appreciate the true threat facing the kingdom until it was too late to save themselves.

King Asparuh, on the other hand, was committed to using all of his power to put down any who threatened to revolt and transform his kingdom into a perfect society.

With the pleasantries out of the way, it was now time for the king and me to discuss serious matters.

"Thank you for making these arrangements with Rhoden and Canada, Arc. If it weren't for your efforts, our fine kingdom would be lost."

This caused a stir among the king's guards.

"All I did was express your wishes. It is the parties involved who have come together to help one another out. Princess Riel deserves praise for having sought us out in the first place."

A smile sprang to the king's lips. "You're right. My

daughter has certainly done more than her fair share. Speaking of which, where is Riel?"

"She is safe and sound in the Rhoden Kingdom. I will bring her back here with the Rhoden forces shortly. It seems that she and her royal counterpart have gotten along quite well."

King Asparuh seemed relieved. "Well, I'm happy to hear that she's made friends outside of the castle. I'll leave Riel to you for now. Good luck in the upcoming battle, Arc. Our fate is in your hands."

The king bowed, then left with his honor guard. There was still much to do to get the grounds ready to take in another 10,000 soldiers.

I made my way back to the teleportation spot. "Back to work, I suppose."

"Kyii!" Ponta agreed from atop my head.

Feeling slightly re-energized, I told Dillan that I'd be heading back to Maple and used Transport Gate again, this time just with Ponta.

An instant later, I was back in the stadium. At the behest of one of the high elders, the next group of soldiers swarmed me.

Once again, I was overcome with the feeling of being on a morning commuter train. I teleported the next group back to the Nohzan Kingdom.

This was a far greater burden on my body than I'd originally anticipated, and I felt sudden guilt over how I'd taken the elven transportation industry for granted. But that didn't stop me from traveling back and forth, like a piston running on automatic.

Fortunately, all that hard work paid off. Just before noon, I finished teleporting the last of the soldiers over to Nohzan. It had taken around fifty trips, and had certainly been a lot of work, but magically and physically speaking, I was far from spent.

Briahn and the rest of the high elders seemed impressed.

Ariane, who'd chosen to remain with me, suggested I take a brief break. "Thanks, Arc. Why don't we have lunch, and then we can tackle the Rhoden Kingdom this afternoon?"

Chiyome had stayed in the Nohzan Kingdom with the last group, though apparently, she hadn't been able to make contact with Goemon and the others yet.

I wasn't really too worried about them though. Goemon was as tough as nails.

"Well, we'd better eat a hearty lunch and build up our strength."

"Kyii! Kyiiiii!"

I rolled my shoulders to try and work out some of the stiffness that had crept in from all the teleporting.

After leaving the stadium and heading into the city proper, I asked Ariane where we should eat. "Any lunch suggestions?"

She offered me an annoyed frown. "I mean, there are a ton of good places. We could be here all day if you want me to rattle off suggestions for—"

Before Ariane had a chance to finish this sentence, Eevin appeared out of nowhere and wrapped her arms tightly around her sister from behind. "Ariiiiiiin! Come to lunch with meeee!"

"Eevin?! What're you...?!"

"Now, listen. I know you don't have a lot of time, so hurry up and let's go."

Eevin urged Ariane on in a sugary sweet tone, all while giving me a death glare.

She apparently had what could be charitably described as a sister complex, and didn't take kindly to my being here.

"Now, hold on a second. You're supposed to be in charge of the civil defenses, remember?! Arc, get over here!"

Ariane shot me a desperate look as she tried fending off her sister. I could tell that their relationship would become an issue in the future.

After a tense lunch, we finally managed to convince Eevin to return to her duty, though she pouted the whole time as she waved goodbye.

Ariane looked exhausted from all the attention and let out a loud sigh as soon as her sister was out of earshot. She then rapped her knuckles on my armor.

"All right, break time's over. Time to head to Rhoden. Riel's waiting on us."

I nodded. "You're right."

"Kyiii..." Ponta mewed and raised a paw in agreement, lulled into a lazy daze by the large lunch.

Worried that Ponta might not be able to hold on while napping, I took the fox off my head and handed it to Ariane. The two of us stepped close, Ponta let out a loud yawn from between Ariane's arms, and I summoned up Transport Gate.

An instant later, we were standing before a large group of soldiers, outfitted and ready to go. Princess Riel Nohzan Saureah and her two bodyguards, Zahar and Niena, were waiting with them.

As soon as the young princess caught sight of us, she immediately started jogging in our direction.

"You're late, Arc! We've been worried sick!"

The eleven-year-old princess stood around 140 centimeters tall, and had bright blonde hair that bounced around her shoulders as she ran. Her youthful exuberance shone through in nearly everything she did.

But looking closer, I saw concern in her eyes.

It was understandable, of course. Transporting these troops out to her homeland could mean the difference between life and death for her people. Despite her young age, she'd been entrusted with organizing the reinforcements from the Rhoden Kingdom and the Great Canada Forest.

Riel was more mature than she appeared. She understood all too well what was at stake. Such worries had likely contributed to her growing up faster than she might have normally.

I dropped to a knee and tried putting her at ease. "Apologies for causing you such concern, Princess. I finished teleporting all of the reinforcements from Canada without issue. They are waiting for us in Nohzan. Everything is going according to plan."

Riel let out a sigh of relief. "I'm glad to hear that."

A voice interrupted our exchange. "I'm sure with power like his, a slight delay would hardly be a concern. Indeed, rushing like this hurts our ability to properly prepare for battle, Princess."

The man was Sekt Rondahl Karlon Rhoden Sahdiay, prince of the Rhoden Kingdom.

Tall, handsome, and with light brown hair, Prince Sekt was dressed in elaborately decorated armor. He looked like the kind of prince you'd read about in fairytales.

Though still young, in his early twenties at the oldest, he had the intense demeanor of royalty. His sneering, insincere greeting did little to strengthen the image of a gentle prince that he tried to convey.

There was something I didn't like about him, though I couldn't quite put my finger on what it was.

A few moments later, a young woman with blonde, wavy hair and dressed in a regal gown stepped up to his side.

Yuriarna Merol Melissa Rhoden Olav, princess of the Rhoden Kingdom, was Sekt's younger sister.

Her eyes were brown, her gaze friendly, belying a strength that rested just beneath the surface.

"That's a bit much, don't you think, Sekt? Riel... I mean, Princess Riel is worried about the future of her kingdom. It's entirely understandable that she would want to hurry things along. Don't you agree, Arc?"

Princess Yuriarna glanced over at her brother.

I got the sense that the two didn't have the best relationship.

I wasn't in a hurry to side with either of them at this point, and I stumbled over my words for a moment in the hopes of finding some way out of the situation. I glanced at Ariane, only to find her looking off in another direction, a dozing Ponta in her arms.

The only option was to change the topic of conversation.

"Before I transport the soldiers here to Nohzan, I would like to speak with the king, if I may. Is he available?"

I hadn't exactly been expecting the king himself to see us off, but it did seem a bit odd for him to not make an appearance before sending his own son to war.

Princess Yuriarna replied first. "There was a bit of a commotion in the capital this morning, so father is working on getting that under control."

Her voice sounded odd as she explained this, but I wasn't sure why. She couldn't seem to hold my gaze, looking away from time to time.

Sekt shrugged his shoulders and shot his sister a sarcastic grin. "Turns out there were quite a few people in Rhoden who were breaking the law and using elves for labor, so I hope you appreciate this as a sign of our loyalty."

Ariane and I exchanged a confused look.

Princess Riel stood on her toes in an attempt to look taller as she joined the conversation. "Early this morning, while we were still sleeping, two giant dragons flew over the city. Zahar heard the commotion and went outside to look, but they were already gone. Apparently, the king got to speak with them. I really wish I could've talked to a dragon."

Niena frowned at her young charge's disappointment. She took a knee in front of Riel.

"That's not possible, my princess. No matter how intelligent the dragon might be, it's too great a danger for you to go near one. Just think how brokenhearted the king would be if something happened to you."

I leaned over to Ariane and whispered in her ear. "Do you suppose one of the dragons was Felfi Visrotte?"

She shook her head.

Now, I wasn't exactly well-versed in the different types of dragons living in this world, but the only ones I knew of that could speak were the Dragon Lords. Ariane seemed to be thinking the same thing.

But even if it had been Felfi Visrotte, when we'd parted ways with her this morning, she was alone.

The only thing I could think of was that she'd reached out to one of the other Dragon Lords in Canada. But then…why were they in Rhoden and not Nohzan, where they were supposed to be heading?

I just couldn't understand why two Dragon Lords, intelligent beings that they were, would come to a city full of humans. From the way Princess Riel made it sound, seeing a dragon up close was an incredibly rare occurrence here.

And not only had the dragons spoken directly to the king before leaving, but they also hadn't done any damage to the castle or surrounding city as far as I could tell.

Prince Sekt seemed to have interpreted the sudden appearance of these dragons as a show of force from Canada, so I figured it wasn't the best time to ask what the king had discussed with them. Besides, it was entirely possible that this meeting had been at the behest of the high elders.

I decided to let the topic drop and move on to other matters. "Well, I think it's about time we made our way to the Nohzan Kingdom. Could you please order all those who will be traveling to form up around me?"

Prince Sekt stepped in close. "Given that I will serve as the representative for the Rhoden Kingdom, I should go first so I can meet with the other parties and make the necessary introductions. I'll also need to bring my personal guard."

I watched as nearly a dozen guards led their horses over to me.

Looking around, I noted that the area was filled with not only soldiers, but also mounted knights and horse-drawn carts laden with supplies. The sheer mass of people and things took up far more space than the elves had.

I began having my doubts about whether we could transport them all with the half day left to us.

"I'm going too!" said Princess Riel. "I need to report back to Father. And besides, I'm worried about my people!"

After Riel and Yuriarna said their goodbyes, the young girl and her bodyguards hurried over to my side.

"I'm counting on you, Arc."

"I know."

I was relieved to realize my first trip of the afternoon wouldn't be a repeat of the cramped train incident from this morning, though it also drove home how inconsiderate I'd been to Fangas and Dillan, asking them to squeeze in tight like that. Fortunately, they didn't seem to have minded.

I shook my head. "All right then, we're off to the Nohzan Kingdom. Please stay inside the rune circle at all times."

As I made this announcement, several of the knights took a few steps back. When I summoned up Transport Gate, I heard yells of surprise. These humans were far more jittery around magic than the elves.

I glanced over at the mountains of supplies and people waiting to be transported and sighed. "I'll be lucky if I'm done by midnight."

Just as the words left my mouth, we were gone.

After seeing Sekt off for his meeting with King Asparuh, I got to work traveling back and forth between Nohzan and Rhoden.

The sky was the color of burnt umber by the time I transported the final group of horse-drawn carts from

Rhoden and left them with their Nohzan attendants. My job finished, I stretched my arms to relieve some of the tension that had built up in my shoulders.

"You know, more than the constant use of magic to teleport people, I think it's the sheer repetition that really makes this exhausting," I muttered aloud to no one in particular.

What had once been a tranquil courtyard near the castle was now filled to the brim with Rhoden soldiers and their supplies, creating a literal tent city.

Having foreign soldiers posted right outside the place where the royal family lived would have been a huge ordeal under normal circumstances, but these were hardly normal circumstances.

Besides, the entire kingdom of Nohzan would have been wiped out if Rhoden hadn't sent reinforcements. In a way, the whole world was rising up in revolt.

Of course, it wasn't only the Rhoden soldiers camping out in the courtyard. A little farther off, the elves were setting up their own tents, giving the whole area the feel of an overgrown summer camp.

As was typical of well-trained soldiers, the people gathered here seemed to be in high spirits about the upcoming battle. I even heard the occasional cheer rising up from the various gatherings.

Whenever I passed a group, they would dutifully stop what they were doing to salute or offer up a greeting. I was starting to feel like a bit of a celebrity—which I really didn't mind at all.

I still hoped to see my idealized fantasy world come true, one in which humans, mountain people, elves, and even dwarves all lived together. If I needed to give everything I had in order to make that a reality, then that was what I intended to do.

Ever since coming here, I'd tried to stay out of the limelight and avoid drawing attention to myself. But I couldn't just watch people suffer in silence.

I had to wonder how many people actually *could*. Living on your own, never interacting with another soul, far from any form of human settlement... That was a lot more work than it might seem.

The longer you lived in a place, the harder it was to cut yourself off from it.

My thoughts were interrupted by a voice behind me. "You did good work back there, Arc."

I turned to find Chiyome. I hadn't seen her since we'd parted earlier this afternoon.

For once, she was walking among humans with her pointed ears and long tail exposed, wagging freely.

"Ah, Chiyome. Were you able to meet up with Goemon?"

She shook her head.

I glanced up at the setting sun. Quite some time had passed since they were supposed to show up. Could something have happened to them?

I felt unease rising inside me. Chiyome's ears were standing at attention as she looked back at me with her azure eyes.

"If I don't hear anything by tomorrow, I'll make my way to Delfrent to try and pick up their trail. Arc, I..."

Before she could continue, a large outcry went up around us. Chiyome and I scanned through the crowd to figure out what was happening.

"What the hell is that?!"

Shouts began erupting from the east, so I turned toward the darkening sky.

There were two shadows flying straight toward the castle at high speed. I could tell they were enormous, even from here. As they drew close, it quickly became evident that our new visitors were dragons.

Though both massive, the one leading was at least double the size of its partner. It was covered in black scales and had violet marks running across its wings, like ripples on a pond. In addition to the two horns sprouting from its head, I also noted that the tip of its tail sparkled in the dying sunlight. Somehow, this dragon felt familiar, even though I knew I'd never set eyes on it before.

The one taking the rear, however, was easy to identify.

Four wings sprouted out of its blue-scaled body, and two horns rose from each side of its head. Not only had I met this dragon on multiple occasions, but I'd actually fought him.

This was undoubtedly Villiers Fim, the Dragon Lord I'd encountered near the forest beyond the Furyu Mountains at the base of the Lord Crown. Which meant that the huge dragon—a Dragon Lord, maybe?—leading him toward us must have been none other than...

"Is that... Is that bigger one up there Felfi Visrotte?"

I'd never seen her as a dragon, but when I recalled her humanoid form, it made sense. Felfi Visrotte had decided to bring Villiers Fim along to boost our firepower.

I knew that Villiers Fim was smitten with Felfi Visrotte, a fact that she was also all too aware of. Perhaps she'd decided to take advantage of this.

"Looks like we've gained another powerful ally."

Chiyome gazed up at the eastern sky, her tail wagging excitedly. I nodded in agreement.

While these two Dragon Lords would be a great help in keeping the undead armies at bay, the soldiers around us didn't seem to share in our excitement. They began arming themselves, moving away from their carts while their commanders started to shout orders.

Unlike the elves, humans rarely ever saw Dragon Lords.

My mind raced as I tried thinking of a way to calm the agitated crowd, but before I had a chance to act, I heard a series of loud trumpet blasts from the direction of the castle. The pattern repeated several times.

The soldiers looked confused, but they slowly began putting down their weapons, and the tension started to ease.

The two Dragon Lords slowed as they drew near, their powerful wings sending blasts of wind down onto everyone and everything below. They landed in a corner of the castle's courtyard.

Ariane and Fangas were probably going to meet with them immediately, so I figured I should be there too.

"Shall we get going, Chiyome?"

Her ears perked up as she glanced in another direction. "Go on without me. I have to meet with someone else."

She disappeared into the crowd of bewildered soldiers. Judging by how she was acting, I couldn't help but wonder if she'd somehow received word from Goemon. My senses were nowhere near as good as hers, so I easily could have missed some signal.

I stood there for a few moments, hoping she'd show back up, but it quickly became clear that that wasn't going to happen. I headed toward the elven side of the encampment.

Though the space reserved for the elves was quite a bit smaller than the one for the Rhoden Kingdom, this was logistical and not a question of the Nohzan Kingdom giving humans preferential treatment. The elves simply hadn't brought as much stuff as the Rhoden reinforcements.

The space was quite cramped with two dragons sitting in the middle of it.

The Dragon Lord that I assumed to be Felfi Visrotte was about eighty meters in length, and the sheer immensity of her body grew all the more intimidating the closer I drew. However, I also noticed that both Dragon Lords appeared to be shrinking as I approached, until they'd completely transformed into their humanoid forms.

They looked just like two people standing in the middle of a large gathering of elven soldiers.

One of the figures was, indeed, Felfi Visrotte, in the same form she'd been in when we fought.

She stabbed the crystalline tip of her large, serpentine tail into the ground and ran a hand through her violet hair.

Next to her, standing at around four meters tall, was Villiers Fim. Though his body was humanoid in shape, his height was a dead giveaway that he was anything but human. His dragon head and blue scales further confirmed this.

I was surprised to see that Villiers Fim was twice the size of Felfi Visrotte in their humanoid forms—a complete reversal from when they were dragons.

Felfi Visrotte grinned. "Heya, Arc! Sorry to make you wait like that."

I weaved my way through the soldiers until I arrived in front of her. A moment later, Ariane showed up with five other figures in tow.

Accompanying Ariane were representatives from the united armies: Fangas and Dillan from Canada, Prince Sekt from Rhoden, and King Asparuh and Princess Riel from Nohzan.

Ariane adjusted Ponta in her arms and nodded in my direction before making her way to the Dragon Lords.

"You must have had a long journey."

Felfi Visrotte smiled back at Ariane and gave a dismissive wave of her hand. "You must be the little sister Eevin talks about so much. Ariane, right? Anyway, I figured the more power we have, the better, so I dragged this guy along. You don't mind, right?"

Villiers Fim seemed to physically shrink as he shrugged his shoulders and glanced about nervously.

You'd think he'd be a little more grandiose about the fact that he'd come all the way out here to join a battle to save humans, but I got the sense that the circumstances around his coming here weren't all that they appeared to be.

Despite his massive body, he was squirming around like a new recruit.

"It's a great honor to hear that Villiers Fim has also agreed to join the fight. I assume your delay was due to a trip to the Furyu Mountains? I would've figured it was a mere twenty-minute flight from Maple."

Felfi Visrotte had implied that the reason for her delay was Villiers Fim, but something didn't add up. Especially not with the way he was acting.

Flying across the Great Canada Forest from Maple to the Furyu Mountains and on to the shrine beyond, followed by crossing the mountains again to travel all the way to the Nohzan Kingdom, would certainly have been quite a journey, even if I couldn't say exactly how far.

But even so, it should only have taken about half a day to cover the distance. I had no doubt that flying was the fastest mode of transport in this world—aside from my teleportation magic.

Felfi Visrotte belted out a laugh. "Well, y'see, I got a little confused and ended up in the wrong country entirely. I really can't tell one human kingdom from the next, or even where they are."

The representatives of the three countries looked shocked at her answer.

Apparently, she'd gotten caught up in the excitement of it all and had just taken off without bothering to ask for directions. This made sense, given the stories we'd heard earlier about the king of Rhoden suddenly having to entertain a pair of dragons.

But had she really been lost, or was there something else going on here?

Fangas spoke up next, a cheerful lilt to his husky voice. "Well, I truly appreciate you coming all the way out here, Felfi Visrotte." He turned to the other Dragon Lord. "And Villiers Fim, I've heard much about you from my granddaughter. I cannot properly express just how honored we are that you would join us in battle."

Villiers Fim looked down at Fangas sheepishly. "W-well, since Felfi Visrotte wanted me here, I could hardly turn her down. Ah... Ahaha!"

Though they were both Dragon Lords, Villiers Fim seemed to be in absolute awe of Felfi Visrotte. He was acting completely different from his usual, confident self. It was clear he wasn't used to being around people.

I looked from Felfi Visrotte to Fangas and back to

try and glean a little more context about what was going on here, but their expressions were completely neutral. Out of the corner of my eye, I caught sight of Prince Sekt scowling as he listened to the conversation.

King Asparuh spoke next. "I am truly honored that you have agreed to come out here and assist our country in its darkest hour. I would like to offer my thanks to you on behalf of all of the people of Nohzan." With that out of the way, he got down to business. "I have made arrangements to conduct a joint planning meeting back at the castle. Please, follow me."

Felfi Visrotte threw out her arms and stretched. "Well, thank God for that. I'm all tuckered out after such a long flight. I'd love to sit down for a bit."

She was about to start off when she stopped and looked back over her shoulder, as if suddenly remembering something.

"Y'know, I think Villy's gonna have a bit of a hard time squeezing in there. Why don't you be a good boy and wait here for us?"

Felfi Visrotte glanced at me before making her way toward the castle. Villiers Fim slumped visibly and hung his head at being ordered to stay behind.

I kind of felt bad for the guy, but she was right. Sure, he could probably squeeze himself through the castle interior, but there was no way he'd fit into any chairs or other furnishings with his current size. Staying behind only made sense.

King Asparuh headed for the castle, followed closely by Fangas and Prince Sekt. Before I could join them, Ariane jogged over to me, Ponta dangling from her arms. She glanced around before speaking.

"Where's Chiyome? I thought she said she was going to meet up with you when you got back."

It took me a moment to realize what Ariane was actually asking. "I spoke with Chiyome earlier, but she told me she had to meet up with someone and left very suddenly. I figured she must have sensed that Goemon had finally arrived."

"Kyii! Kyiiiii!"

Out of nowhere, Ponta started mewing anxiously and leaped from Ariane's arms up to my helmet.

"Whoa, what's up little buddy? Did you see something that…?"

Before I could finish, I caught sight of a familiar figure out of the corner of my eye.

Standing at over two meters tall, the muscle-bound figure dressed all in black stood out even among the bustling crowd of elves setting up camp. Atop his head were a pair of cat ears similar to Chiyome's, though his body was covered in a silver and black pattern that made him look like a giant tabby.

This was Goemon, one of the six great fighters of the Jinshin clan. Chiyome walked at his side, along with two more mountain people.

"Ah, Chiyome... Goemon. Glad to see you've arrived safely."

"Hm."

The taciturn cat man responded with a nod and raised his fist in greeting. After bumping fists with him, I greeted his comrades before turning my attention to Chiyome.

"Goemon has provided some good information about what's happening in the Delfrent Kingdom. The capital had already fallen by the time he got there, and the situation is looking pretty bleak."

Goemon punctuated her report with a firm nod.

That confirmed that the two countries bordering the Nohzan Kingdom, Delfrent and Salma, had already fallen. It was now only a matter of time before the hordes descended upon us.

"In that case, I think we should bring Goemon to see the king."

With that, we hurried off.

Margrave Wendly du Brahniey, the man charged with overseeing the last standing territory of the Salma Kingdom, was displeased.

"Dammit! So not only did Salma's capital city fall, but Delfrent's too? How is it that only Nohzan was able to turn back the armies of the Holy Hilk Kingdom?!"

The margrave boasted the body of a man who'd grown up in the military, his muscular frame, receding silver hair, and intense gaze giving him an intimidating air—a far cry from most nobility.

He glared down at the map laid out on the table.

Saureah, the capital of the Nohzan Kingdom, sat right in the center, with Delfrent and Salma near the edges. Two black tokens sat on Larisa and Lione, their respective capitals, while another two marked the Nohzan Kingdom and the Holy Hilk Kingdom.

Fangas crossed his arms and tilted his head back. "It's only a matter of time until we're attacked on three sides."

King Asparuh let out a heavy sigh and slowly shook his head. Princess Riel looked up at her father, the worry written on her young face.

Dillan spoke up next, a deep crease etching his forehead. "If it weren't for Arc here, the capital would have surely fallen and the truth behind the Holy Hilk Kingdom's assault would still be unknown."

Prince Sekt, the man charged with overseeing all of the forces of the Rhoden Kingdom, nodded. "And it's also to Arc's credit that we all find ourselves gathered in this room today. I, for one, am honored by the opportunity to stand among these mystical creatures, whom I'd assumed to be the stuff of legends. The world truly is much smaller than I'd imagined."

He glanced over at Felfi Visrotte and then right above my head as he spoke.

Felfi Visrotte closed her eyes and smiled, letting her long, crystal-tipped tail sway gently back and forth. "The way I see it, you people only inhabit a small part of this great world."

Her reptilian pupils stared out through half-lidded eyes. Everyone in the room shifted uncomfortably at this, which caused her smile to grow even brighter. Sekt swallowed audibly.

They knew in their hearts that what she said was true. The idea that the world revolved around them was pure delusion.

"Kyii!"

Growing antsy at the sudden change in mood, Ponta hopped from my helmet and down to my shoulder before wrapping itself around my neck like a scarf. Felfi Visrotte chuckled at Ponta's reaction before casting her gaze back down to the three tokens sitting atop the map on the table.

"Well, look at that. So I guess all we need to do is wipe out the armies at each of these three spots, yeah? If we assign me, Villy, and Arc each to one of them, we should be all right, yeah? You guys can hang back and catch any that make it through."

The humans in the room looked completely taken aback at such a basic plan, while the elves nodded in agreement.

With a Dragon Lord on the battlefield, there was little need to formulate for an overly complicated strategy. The real problem would be in figuring out how to coordinate the remaining forces.

There was a certain logic to it. With powerhouses like the Dragon Lords and myself involved, there would be far fewer casualties, if we were able to wipe out huge swaths of the enemy.

The only problem with this plan was timing.

I clenched my hand into a fist. "Time is of the essence. Since we're dealing with undead, the longer we wait, more of their victims are likely to rise up and swell their ranks. However, if we were to attack the enemies at their strongholds, we'd risk killing any survivors still holding out."

This wasn't mere boasting. Using the powers of my Paladin class, I could wipe out an entire army of the dead with relative ease. Though I'd rather not go through the experience of using that kind of power again, we didn't have much of a choice right now.

The problem, however, was that there was no way to direct or limit the damage of such a powerful attack. I figured this was also true for the Dragon Lords.

Dillan grabbed a white token sitting off to the side of the map.

"True. These are all the capital cities of their respective countries, right? So I have to imagine that they're at least as big as the city we find ourselves in currently. If there are any survivors within the cities, they'd almost certainly be wiped out in an attack."

Fangas picked up where Dillan had left off. "On the other hand, wiping the other countries off the map would also save us from worrying about any new undead cropping up."

He let out a loud belly laugh, though the look of horror on King Asparuh's face made it clear that not everyone in the room appreciated this dark humor.

"We could hardly do something like that! Who knows what sort of ill will that would give rise to? Even if we managed to destroy all of the undead, we'd risk deepening human distrust toward the elves."

Fangas smiled at this, but said no more.

After a few moments of silence, Dillan tried to allay the King's concerns. "Please, Fangas, this is no time for teasing. We're here to formulate a strategy for battle that will also help build a stronger relationship between us and the humans."

Princess Riel broke out into a smile.

Dillan continued. "Anyway, back to the subject at hand. We need to wipe out the undead armies as soon as possible, before they have a chance to grow any further. We also need to leave the cities largely intact. The way I see it, that means sending our troops to each city's perimeter, to draw the enemy out. Once they're outside the walls, we shouldn't have to worry about any collateral damage."

As he spoke, Dillan placed two white tokens on the map, one in Delfrent and one in Salma.

Prince Sekt was the first to object to this plan. "Undead, even in large groups, lack any sort of consciousness outside of a desire to kill the living. I highly doubt they'd be concerned about a siege. Moreover, these undead are under the direct control of the Holy Hilk Kingdom. So what makes you think they'll fall into our trap?"

Dillan seemed to have anticipated such a question and reached for a black token.

"As you said, undead under intelligent control make for rather deadly opponents. However, as far as I've heard from those who've had personal experience, the Hilk's hold over the undead is tenuous at best."

He paused and looked at each person in the room, until all eyes were on him, urging him to continue.

"Considering that the undead are a type of evil spirit that takes possession of bodies, the energy they thrive on is weakest during the day, while at night, they grow more powerful. I'm sure none of this is news to you."

The elves and mountain people in the room nodded as if this were obvious. The humans, however, seemed surprised.

To be fair, so was I. But at least I had a helmet to cover my reaction.

"However," Dillan continued, "I've been told that the undead that laid siege to this city managed to maintain the assault even through the day and lost much of their focus at night. Judging from this, I think it's safe to say that whoever is controlling them is unable to maintain that control at night, when the undead grow stronger. I can't say why that would be—maybe due to the sheer number they're trying to control—but ultimately, the result is the same."

Prince Sekt, who'd been watching Dillan with great

interest, piped up. "So, if whoever's in charge of these armies loses control at night, then that means they wouldn't be able to mount an effective strategy against us."

Dillan nodded and set another white token down on the map. "That's correct. The longer we wait, the more powerful our enemy becomes, so I believe we should strike out at once. We can split our forces and head to both Salma and Delfrent for a simultaneous attack."

King Asparuh broke his silence, a look of concern on his face. "If we split all of our forces, then who will be left to defend Saureah?"

It was only natural that protecting the capital from another invasion took priority over the king's desire to see the Holy Hilk Kingdom fall.

Dillan looked back down at the map and stroked his beard. "I believe your guards should be sufficient for now. Even if you were invaded again from the west, it would take a considerable amount of time for the troops to arrive. Also, I believe you said your son, Prince Terva, is mustering forces from the surrounding nobles. That should be enough to hold off another siege, no?" He looked around the table.

"Fine by me."

"No arguments here."

"Hmph."

One by one, everyone in the room agreed to his plan, until finally his gaze fell on me. He smiled. "All right then. Arc will take care of the teleporting tomorrow morning."

I was hardly surprised. At this point, I pretty much expected it, even if I wasn't exactly a fan of the slog involved in transporting troops back and forth. There was, however, an issue with this.

"I don't mind teleporting the armies to their positions, but I need to have an image of the place I want to go to firmly in mind in order to teleport there. I've never been to either Salma or Delfrent."

Dillan's eyes went wide. Apparently, this had completely slipped his mind.

I looked down at the map and traced my finger from Saureah to Larisa to Lione. "It'd take me at least a day, maybe two, to get close enough to the capital to teleport people there, and that's just for one of them. I'd need two to four days to travel to both."

According to the map, they were both about equal distance from Saureah. Assuming I had a perfect line of sight and could continuously teleport the whole way, I could maybe make it to one in a single day.

Dillan followed my finger as it moved across and map and furrowed his brow. "Figuring in a little wiggle room, how about three days? I hate to give the enemy more time to bolster its forces, but we don't have any other choice."

He stared darkly at the black tokens sitting on the map.

Felfi Visrotte, who'd been watching this whole exchange with a bemused look, crossed her arms and smirked. "Y'know, I have an even better idea. Wanna hear it?"

She cocked her head to the side and shot me a smile.

The Lost Dragon Lord

$\mathcal{T}$HE LORD CROWN stood prominently atop the mountain, competing with the sky itself for attention. From its massive roots to its thick, leafy canopy, the entire thing was filled to the brim with spirits.

Somehow, as if by a miracle, streaks of light managed to punch their way through the dense foliage to illuminate the path below.

Due to its secluded location, humans never ventured this far. Silence reigned supreme. The only sounds were those of wind rustling the leaves and water lapping in the distance.

Long ago, this place had served as a base of sorts for the mountain people, though now all that remained were the moss-covered ruins of a shrine, illuminated by the scant light that made it down to ground level.

The burbling sounds of a hot spring mingled with the whisper of the leaves, adding to the serenity of the scene.

Though left unused for generations, the large outdoor bath continued filling with naturally heated water, the excess liquid pouring off the edge in a steaming waterfall.

And yet, this mystical place had also fallen into neglect, the pool filling with rotting leaves and the bathhouse descending into decay.

At least, that was the case until quite recently.

A pair of elves and one of the mountain people had begun traveling to this place and improving the facilities, restoring them to their former glory. The place had become so clean that you could count the number of leaves marring the surface of the pool on one hand, and even those eventually joined the water on its trip over the waterfall.

A lone figure sat in the bath, letting the heat permeate his body as his warm breath mixed with the rising steam. As far as he was concerned, there was nothing better than lazing about in a nice, clean bath.

If you were to ask a layperson what this thirty-meter-long, four-winged beast was, you'd almost certainly be told it was a dragon. It was a fair guess, after all, with his blue scales, his four horns, and the striped pattern running down his neck.

More specifically, however, he was a Dragon Lord, a species known for their intellect, long lifespans, and power. They were, both literally and figuratively, at the top of the food chain.

And yet, in spite of all that, Dragon Lord Villiers Fim preferred to spend his days alone, avoiding interacting with outsiders as best he could.

There was one exception, however. One day, a strange elf decked out in full armor had invaded the Dragon Lord's domain. The two had fought briefly before managing to find common ground. Part of their agreement, as requested by the odd-looking elf, was that he would be allowed to use this hot spring whenever he liked.

Villiers Fim yawned lazily in the warm water, wondering whether the armored elf would make an appearance today, when he suddenly sensed a powerful presence drawing near. He stuck his head up out of the water and looked around.

"Who's there?" Even as the words left his mouth, he already suspected who it might be. He shook his head, trying to dispel the notion. That was impossible.

At first, he'd thought it might be the elf, Arc Lalatoya. But Arc always teleported directly to the shrine. That wouldn't explain this approaching power.

Villiers Fim could feel the great force drawing nearer

and nearer, though he couldn't get a grasp on exactly what it was. It was like trying to catch a fistful of fog. Whatever the approaching entity was, it was immense and brimming with energy.

If Villiers Fim had to guess, it was another Dragon Lord.

He glanced toward the Lord Crown and narrowed his eyes, willing the sky into focus. In the distance, he finally caught sight of the source of all this power.

The figure shot through the dense cover above, stirring up a storm of leaves. It was definitely a Dragon Lord, as he'd predicted, but he was taken aback by the sight of exactly *which* Dragon Lord it was. He'd seen those beautiful wings many times from afar; they belonged to Felfi Visrotte, the Dragon Lord based near the center of the Great Canada Forest.

She was at least twice his size and covered in pitch-black scales. With every heavy beat of her mammoth wings, the violet patten on the membranes shimmered beautifully. Looking closer, he saw that her violet eyes were locked straight on his.

The large, crystalline dagger that stuck out of the tip of her tail glinted brilliantly in the sunlight as it traced a slow arc in the air above.

Villiers Fim adjusted his posture and swallowed hard.

He could practically feel her gaze burning a hole straight through him.

From a distance, it might have looked like the Dragon Lord was calm as he watched this newcomer, but inside, he was anything but. His mind raced as he tried to figure out what she was doing here.

The first possibility was that maybe, just maybe, Arc had made good on his promise to deliver Villiers Fim's message asking for an audience with Felfi Visrotte.

But even if that were the case, it didn't explain why she would leave her domain to come all the way to him. His mind continued racing, until she landed heavily at the edge of the pool.

Her voice broke the silence. "So, what should I say? I guess 'hi' would do for a start, huh?"

Even such a simple greeting from this powerful Dragon Lord was enough to cause Villiers Fim to tense up. He knelt before her.

"I'm sure you already know who I am, but for the sake of formalities, let's get it over with. I'm Felfi Visrotte, the Dragon Lord of the Columbia Mountains in the Great Canada Forest. I heard from a man named Arc that you're looking for me?"

She gave Villiers Fim a quick once-over from head to tail before giving a quiet, triumphant nod.

"I'm gonna be generous here and overlook the round-about way you contacted me. Besides, I have a favor I'd like to ask you."

She bared her fangs in what was meant to be a smile.

Being asked for a favor by the great Felfi Visrotte, a Dragon Lord Villiers Fim had admired for years, was nothing short of amazing. Saying "no" never even crossed his mind.

"I will do anything in my power to be of assistance to you."

Felfi Visrotte seemed pleased at this, even though she'd known he'd accept before coming here anyway.

"Well, that's good to know. It's really not a huge deal anyway."

Though they might both have been Dragon Lords, Felfi Visrotte was one of the oldest of their kind and had earned a great deal of respect among the rest of the Dragon Lords—particularly from Villiers Fim.

Felfi Visrotte swung her large tail about gleefully as she stared down at the Dragon Lord kneeling before her... and at the large pool of steaming water around him.

"Well, well, whaddya got here? Pretty rare to see a hot spring out in the middle of nowhere. Did you make this?"

She glanced at her surroundings with great interest and noticed the troughs carved into the surface of the rock to allow cool water to flow in and maintain the water's temperature, as well as the stone tiling beautifully laid out both in and around the pool.

"This was built many generations ago, when the mountain people still called this place home, though Arc has recently been making use of it again. I must admit, it's quite an impressive sight to behold."

Villiers Fim stepped out of the pool and off to the side to make way for her, though there was simply no way that an eighty-meter dragon could have fit in it comfortably.

"Hunh. The only place I've ever seen a hot spring was out near the base of the Karyu Mountains. Well, I've got a little time to kill, so I don't see the harm in taking a dip."

She shook her massive body several times, and it began transforming. Within about five minutes, Felfi Visrotte had shrunk herself down into a two-meter-tall humanoid figure. She then stepped into the warm water.

"Aaaaah, now that feels greeeeat. If I'd known you had a hot spring, I might've stopped by more often."

Villiers Fim's blue scales took on a faint scarlet hue, his tail waving about excitedly. He'd always been hesitant to reach out to her, so hearing her say that she'd actually want to come and visit his domain was like a dream come true.

Felfi Visrotte giggled at the other Dragon Lord's barely contained exuberance.

Villiers Fim noticed his tail wagging and tried to deflect attention away from himself. "Th-that's a pretty impressive transformation there. I'm still not able to shrink myself down that small, nor can I take on the appearance of a human."

Though all Dragon Lords possessed the same ability, how well they were able to pull this off differed from one to the next, largely due to the environment they lived in.

Moreover, transforming into a humanoid was more of a creature comfort, and squeezing their large bodies into such small forms wasn't a skill that could be mastered without a great deal of practice. Felfi Visrotte's humanoid form was evidence of her diligent study.

She looked surprised. "Hmm, is that so? Well, you're still a little kid, really, so I'm sure you'll get it in time. One of these days, maybe you'll have a chance to show it off to me."

Villiers Fim's tail once again started wagging excitedly before he caught himself and quickly changed the subject again. "What is it you would like my help with?"

Felfi Visrotte slumped back luxuriously and raised her tail above the surface of the water to point its crystalline tip at Villiers Fim.

"Ah, that's right. I didn't actually come for the hot spring." She stood up in the pool and smiled at the other

Dragon Lord. "I'm here to ask you for help taking out some bad guys, Villy."

Questions darted through Villiers Fim's mind, though he wasn't about to go back on his word now. He simply nodded in assent.

A short time later, the two were flying through wispy white clouds, watching snow-capped mountain peaks pass beneath them. They were currently over the range that the humans and elves referred to as the Furyu Mountains. On the other side lay what looked like a huge gash in the vast, open plains.

Felfi Visrotte's large wings swept elegantly through the air as she looked down at the terrain below. "That's gotta be the Dragon Wonder, so maybe a little further south?"

Villiers Fim followed her lead as his mind ran over their earlier conversation about the upcoming battle.

"Y'see, Villy, these elves have been a great help to me, and they needed a favor. I agreed to assist them with some pact they made with the humans, but I think it's gonna end up being a pretty big job. I was hoping you could lend me a hand."

He was taken aback when she'd told him the details. Apparently, they were being called upon to wipe out an army of the undead numbering in the hundreds of thousands. There was no way such an army could have come together through natural means.

Absent an undead dragon, creatures of this sort posed little threat to Dragon Lords. Still, Villiers Fim disdained the undead on the grounds that they were abominations of nature. They only existed by abusing the natural flow of spiritual energy. Any time an undead creature happened to wander near Villiers Fim's domain, he took it out with extreme prejudice.

A situation like this was bad enough on its face, but Villiers Fim found himself even more disturbed at the idea that someone was out there *creating* undead, which was the only explanation for such a massive force. Just imagining the land in front of him covered in moving, rotting corpses was enough to send a chill down his spine.

Villiers Fim didn't hesitate for a moment over agreeing to help Felfi Visrotte, though he did feel a sense of unease when he heard that Arc was involved. Arc often looked like a member of the undead himself, though he clearly possessed a spirit of the living.

Even though there should have been a massive power differential between them, Arc was a force to be reckoned with, a point made even more peculiar by the fact that he'd been involved in calling upon Felfi Visrotte for help.

From what she'd said, it sounded like she'd taken quite a liking to Arc—a fact that Villiers Fim felt somewhat conflicted about.

Before he could dwell too much on that thought, though, Felfi Visrotte called out to him from up ahead.

"Heya, Villy! I hate to ask, but do you know where this Nohzan place is?"

He shook his head.

"Umm, no. I'm afraid I don't know much about the human lands."

"I figured. So...what should we do?"

She didn't seem too upset with his response, though judging by the way she muttered to herself, she was in something of a bind.

As far as he could tell, she didn't have any idea where they were heading. Hoping to come to her rescue, Villiers Fim began scanning the scenery below, looking for anything that might provide a clue.

He wasn't terribly surprised that she didn't know where they were heading. Dragon Lords had little more than a passing knowledge of the human countries. In fact, for a Dragon Lord to engage with the elves as much as she did was rare among their kind.

After scanning their surroundings for a bit, Felfi Visrotte noticed a large shape on the horizon that appeared to be humanmade. "Looks like luck's on our side! Let's hop on down there and ask for directions."

With a few powerful flaps of her wings, she changed directions and began gliding toward the human settlement.

Villiers Fim hurried to keep up with her. "Umm, I don't know if it's such a good idea to just pop in on humans like this!"

They dropped in altitude and sped toward the distant settlement, which appeared to be a sprawling city.

A series of massive walls surrounded it, clearly intended to protect the residents living within. Looking closer, Villiers Fim could see a variety of wooden buildings packed close together, and a large, stone castle at the center.

Though he knew little about humans and the lives they led, he understood that the presence of such a magnificent stone structure meant this was where the king lived. It also meant that the chances of the humans down below reacting negatively to the sudden appearance of two Dragon Lords were quite high.

Not that there was much for Villiers Fim and Felfi Visrotte to fear from humans, of course. But since they were trying to help the humans fight a common enemy, it would reflect poorly on them if they destroyed a human kingdom in the process.

Villiers Fim slowed to get a better look at the city, but Felfi Visrotte continued at full speed toward the castle.

Within moments, the guards standing watch atop the towers started rushing about in panic as they caught sight of the dragons.

After making several lazy loops around the castle, and drawing a fair deal of attention in the process, Felfi Visrotte swooped in and perched on one of the highest balconies. She did her best to avoid causing any damage to the building, despite her massive size.

Villiers Fim was impressed by the sheer finesse with which she was able to move about in her dragon form. Alas, he wasn't quite so confident in his own abilities and landed on one of the perimeter walls. Everything was fine when he set down his left foot, but the moment he put weight on his right, he heard stone crumble beneath him.

He scowled and watched a small landslide tumble down the wall.

"They really should make these things stronger..."

Though he was less than half the size of Felfi Visrotte, at a mere thirty meters long, he had quite a bit of girth to him. Still, it was absolutely amazing to him that she'd managed to land so gently, without causing any damage at all.

Felfi Visrotte peeked through the window, catching sight of a figure moving around inside. "Hey, you there! I've got a quick question. Think you could help me out?"

The figure was dressed in elegant robes and accompanied by a contingent of guards. The moment they spotted the dragon, the guards drew their weapons and placed themselves in front of the figure.

"Protect the king!"

"Secure an escape route!"

"Draw your weapons! Someone call the mages!"

While the soldiers busily prepared themselves for combat, Felfi Visrotte smiled at the knowledge that she'd managed to find the king of this country. His guards, however, misinterpreted her bared teeth as something far more sinister. They raised their weapons, ready to lay down their lives if need be.

As the king was being ushered out of the room, he turned back to look out the window and caught the Dragon Lord's gaze. His sharp blue eyes, set beneath a forehead etched with deep wrinkles, gazed intently at the Dragon Lord.

"Hurry up, Your Highness! We haven't a moment to spare!"

The bodyguards urged the king on, but he raised a hand to silence them. He began making his way toward the Dragon Lord with slow, purposeful steps.

"I am King Karlon Delfriet Rhoden Olav, ruler of the Rhoden Kingdom. I can tell by your attempt not to cause our fair castle any harm that you are here on a mission of goodwill. I will answer your question to the best of my ability."

The guards seemed reassured by the king's demeanor and put away their weapons as they watched in silence, anxious to see what would happen next.

"Rhoden, huh? Y'know, now that you mention it, I remember Eva saying something about a place they had some problems with back when the forest was being occupied. That wasn't you, was it?"

The king's face tensed at this.

"Gyahahaha! Just a little joke, no need to look so scared. Anyway, I'm Felfi Visrotte, one of the Dragon Lords living in the Great Canada Forest. Now, the reason why I'm here is pretty simple, actually. You see, I'm looking for a place called the Nohzan Kingdom, and I seem to have lost my way. I hate to bother you, but could you point me in the right direction?"

All the guards stood stone-faced, exchanging glances with one another at this rather odd request. Was she telling the truth?

If they could have read the sincerity on her face, they would instantly have understood where she was coming from. But of course, trying to decipher a Dragon Lord's expression was beyond the average human.

King Karlon looked straight up at the Dragon Lord perched outside his window. The only logical explanation was that her trip to the Nohzan Kingdom had something to do with their request for reinforcements.

The fact that two Dragon Lords had been sent here from Canada might mean that they were being watched. But the Rhoden Kingdom had learned its lesson long ago, and hadn't entered the Great Canada Forest in generations, though the elves might see this differently, due to their longer lifespans. What was ancient history to the people of the Rhoden Kingdom was still relatively recent to elves and Dragon Lords.

Ultimately, the king decided it best to simply answer her question as directly and honestly as possible.

After getting directions, Felfi Visrotte turned her attention away from him and spread her massive wings.

"Well, let's try to keep things on good terms then, huh? See ya later!"

With that, she took off from the balcony, the downdraft from her wings blasting the occupants of the room. She did a loop around the castle before shooting high into the sky, followed shortly by Villiers Fim.

The two Dragon Lords grew smaller and smaller, until they were lost among the clouds.

The king's guards looked around uncertainly. One of them spoke up.

"Wh-what happened just now, Your Highness?"

The guard sounded worried, though the king attempted to ease her fears with a wave of his hand. The creases in the king's forehead seemed deeper than usual, though a slight grin tugged at the corners of his lips.

The guards felt shame wash over them at how easily they'd fallen into a panic while the king had managed to keep his cool. It didn't speak too highly of their training.

"It seems the castle is in a bit of chaos over the sudden appearance of a Dragon Lord."

"We're on it, Your Highness!"

The guards turned to head out of the room, but the king stopped them.

"No, leave it be for now. I want you to summon Prime Minister Bionissa at once. The citizens of our fair capital almost certainly witnessed this display of power from Canada, so let's use this opportunity to round up those who have been thorns in our sides. Even if we have to get our hands dirty, they'll be too worked up with fear over the elven threat to say much."

Two guards took off down the corridor to summon the prime minister.

"Arc should be here a little after noon. Tell Sekt that I want the soldiers ready to depart without delay."

Another guard ran out of the room to deliver this message to Sekt.

The king gazed out the window and grinned. "Today is shaping up to be quite a busy day."

He turned and left the room, his large cape billowing behind him.

CHAPTER 2

The Pontiff

I T WAS A PERFECT DAY for flying, with nary a cloud in the sky.

Right in front of me, the massive, eighty-meter dragon was crouched low to the ground, watching me with her reptilian eyes.

I hesitantly approached Felfi Visrotte, tilting my head back farther and farther as I drew closer.

"Are you sure about this?"

She narrowed her violet eyes and jerked her chin forward, urging me to hurry up.

"Hey, you were the one complaining about this, right? It'd take too long to teleport there and back, you said. Now hurry up and get on my back so I can fly you out there."

She motioned again for me to climb up on her back.

The night before, we'd decided that I needed to travel to the two locations where we'd be teleporting our split forces to take on the undead armies. After hearing my plan, Felfi Visrotte had suggested that there was a much faster way for me to get there.

Flying on the back of a Dragon Lord would greatly reduce the travel time, since I no longer needed to worry about rivers, mountains, or other place where I'd have a poor line of sight.

Given that the undead armies of the Holy Hilk Kingdom were drawing closer by the minute, it made sense to use whichever method was fastest. However, I still felt my heart race at the very idea of riding on the back of a dragon.

I'd never felt this way, even when riding on my drift-pus, Shiden. But there was something inside me that felt slightly uncomfortable about riding on top of a woman, even if she wasn't actually human.

"Hey, Ariane, Chiyome, do you want to join?"

I called out to my friends in an attempt to make the situation a little more comfortable...and to serve as an emotional buffer.

Ariane shook her head. "I-I think I'm all right here for now. I'd hate to be a bother."

Chiyome's cat ears went flat atop her head and her tail puffed up. She stepped behind Ariane, as if to hide. "Just thinking about flying is scary enough, to be honest."

I shrugged, though I felt a bit dejected. If they didn't want to come, then I certainly wasn't going to force them. I felt Ponta tapping the top of my helmet, as if to encourage me.

"Kyii! Kyiiiii!"

I was happy to have my cheerful little travel companion at least.

"Glad you're coming with me, buddy."

Felfi Visrotte rolled her eyes at my incessant stalling and urged me to hurry up. "Listen, Arc, I don't have time for these stupid games. Hurry up and climb on so we can get going. I need to make sure you don't fall off while we're flying, so I *don't* need any extra people around. It'll just take more time to get up to speed."

She lifted her long tail into the air and swung its crystalline tip around to my lower back, nudging me forward.

She was right, of course. I was the only one who needed to travel to these locations. It wasn't necessary for anyone else to come along.

However, as I looked up at the sea of black scales, I did discover one problem with riding on her back.

Unlike Shiden, who had a saddle for me to hold on to as he ran along, Felfi Visrotte had nothing of the sort on her back.

Not that this was unexpected. Dragon Lords, after all, weren't meant to serve as mounts. In fact, I highly doubted anyone had even dared to try until now. Besides, there wasn't a saddle out there big enough to fit across her body.

To not fall off during flight, I'd just have to act like Ponta did atop of my head: by ducking low and hanging on tight.

I shoved my teleportation diary and something to draw with into a bag and cinched it over my shoulders. Once that was done, I climbed onto Felfi Visrotte's back.

The dark scales had a strange texture to them—hard, yet with a bit of give to them at the same time. Intrigued by this odd sensation, I ran my hand across her glistening hide for a moment, until the Dragon Lord's sharp voice brought me back to reality.

"Stop feeling me up like that, you pervert!"

I immediately stopped what I was doing and offered an apology. "Ah, I'm sorry! I've never felt something quite like this before."

I could sense Ariane glaring daggers at me, but I couldn't bring myself to look at her.

Here I was, claiming I felt weird about climbing on top of a woman, and then the moment I did, massaging her like that. It wasn't my proudest moment. Even I could admit that.

Once I finally got into place atop her back, the elves who'd come to see us off stepped away to give us space. Felfi Visrotte unfurled her wings.

"All right, and we're off! Hang on, and try to not fall!"

"All right, I got iiiiiiiiiit?!"

A beautiful pattern flashed across her wings as she began flapping, and suddenly I was thrown back by the sheer force of her takeoff. It was everything I could do just to hang on.

"Gaaaaaaaaaaaaaaaaaaaaaaaaaaaaaaaaah!!!"

I could hardly hear myself scream over the roar of the wind as we tore through the air. It was a completely bizarre sensation, unlike anything I'd experienced before.

Since simply keeping my grip was a struggle in its own right—and daring to glimpse over the side was out of the question—all I could do was relish the new sensation and watch the sky as we flew. This must have been how astronauts felt as they rode their rockets into space.

"Kyiiiiiiii!"

At least Ponta seemed to be having fun.

I felt a brief wave of jealousy wash over me. However,

after a few more minutes, my body went light and the wind died down.

Sensing this was my chance, I leaned over and looked at the terrain below. The city of Saureah was already a tiny speck.

I had no idea exactly how high we were, but judging by the size of the capital, I figured we had to be one or two thousand meters up.

"We're pr-pretty high! If I fall off now, I'm done for."

"Kyii! Kyiiiii!"

If I'd had skin, I'd almost certainly had been covered in goosebumps.

A new feeling began overtaking me, a sense of excitement at speeding through the air as the beautiful world moved beneath me.

Felfi Visrotte flew easily through the air in a long, lazy turn, putting the sun at our backs as we headed west. Moments later, Saureah was a lost sight, and I found myself looking down at the snow-capped Sobir mountain range that served as the border between the Nohzan and Salma kingdoms.

The mountains themselves were quite large, so we had to be at least 3,000 meters above ground by now in order to clear them with ease. However, Felfi Visrotte continued climbing higher into the sky as we flew.

"Well, this will definitely get us to the Salma capital in no time."

Ponta slowly crawled out of its hiding place in the crook of my arm and let its large tail unfurl and billow in the wind.

"Kyii! Kyiiiii!"

Felfi Visrotte tilted her long neck to glance back at me and smiled. "Of course we will. You're flying with me, after all. And hey, I even made sure to check a map this time, so you've got nothing to worry about. Just sit back, relax, and enjoy the view!"

Outside of my long-distance teleportation magic, this was the fastest method of travel by far. It was a shame we couldn't transport all 10,000 soldiers like this.

Although, judging by the way the others had reacted to the suggestion, there was more than a little hesitation about transporting people by Dragon Lord.

Not only was there the issue of having to endure the sheer cold that accompanied being up so high and flying at such great speeds, but it also took quite a bit of strength to hang on during takeoff and even throughout the flight. It was probably for the better that Ariane and Chiyome hadn't come along.

Felfi Visrotte probably knew this too, which is why she'd objected to bringing anyone else along. Though, it did make me wonder how she'd known that *I* would be able to hang on. Perhaps she hadn't and it was simply a risk she'd been willing to take.

In any case, that left teleportation as our only option to get 10,000 soldiers where they needed to go.

Ponta was the real trooper here, though. It was having a great time speeding through the air and letting its long, cottony tail billow in the wind.

After a short while, Felfi Visrotte called out from up ahead. "Hey, Arc, you're pretty quiet back there. Would you mind talking about something to keep me entertained?"

I was perfectly satisfied just sitting quietly and taking in the sights, but apparently, she was looking for conversation.

I hesitated, unsure what to talk about with her. I finally settled on the topic of the first time we'd met.

"Do you mind if I ask you a question?"

"Of course not. Whatcha got?"

While I was certainly impressed with her appearance the first time we'd met, there was something that had struck me as even more interesting: her accent.

Since Villiers Fim was the first Dragon Lord I'd ever met, I kind of assumed that all Dragon Lords spoke in the same formal manner he did. I couldn't get over the unique, casual way Felfi Visrotte spoke.

Since no one else had said anything about it, though, I'd just let it go, until now.

"You have a rather unique way of speaking, so I was wondering if you've always had an accent. Or maybe Villiers Fim is actually the one who speaks strangely?"

She blinked her large, violet eyes at me several times before bursting into laughter. "Gyahahahaha! *That's* what you wanna know? You really must be from the other world then, huh?"

She faced forward again before continuing. "Y'see, Eva was the one who taught me how to speak your language, so I guess I just picked up her accent."

She cocked her head, as if unsure how to provide a more definitive answer.

"Hmm, I guess that makes sense..."

Now that I thought about it, her accent had a slight twang to it that resembled the way people from Kyoto spoke. Not exactly spot on, but close. But just what had she and the founding elder talked about anyway?

I'd always kind of figured that Evanjulin, the founding elder of the Great Canada Forest, was Canadian. But from the way Felfi Visrotte spoke, it now sounded possible that Evanjulin might have been Japanese.

"Kyii! Kyiiiii!" Ponta mewed excitedly as it looked over the Dragon Lord's side at the world passing below.

Its fluffy tail whipped about in the powerful gusts of wind.

I leaned over to see what had gotten Ponta so excited only to find that we were now past the Sobir Mountains and flying over vast, open plains—the lands of the Salma Kingdom.

"Looks like we've crossed the border already. That really was fast!"

"If I recall correctly, the capital city of this country is called Larisa, and it should be right on the water."

Before leaving Saureah, Felfi Visrotte had looked over some maps to get the lay of the land. Fortunately, it seemed to have worked, as she had a pretty good understanding of where we were.

The plains below us seemed almost endless...until I caught sight of a body of water on the horizon. That must be the South Central Sea.

I felt relief wash over me. We'd made it here in less than a half a day. At this rate, our original battle plan might still work.

In the distance, I could just make out a port city surrounded by a massive wall. In the middle was a large fort that sat atop a hill, giving it an imposing view of surrounding lands. According to the description given by Margrave Brahniey, this was Larisa, the capital of the Salma Kingdom.

Felfi Visrotte began her descent as we approached our objective. The closer we got, the more detail I could make out. It rapidly became clear that things were not right with the city.

All of the boats docked at the pier had either been destroyed, and were sitting low in the water, or they were on fire, sending billowing smoke high into the air.

A little further off, I spied several other ships floating aimlessly in the bay, but almost all of their masts were too damaged to serve any purpose.

The city itself was a scene of destruction, flames running rampant through the remnants of once-great neighborhoods.

The messenger from Larisa who'd met with the margrave had told the truth: The city had fallen to a massive army of undead.

From this distance, it was impossible to tell if there were any survivors.

After giving the city a quick look over, Felfi Visrotte twisted her neck and looked back at me.

"There are a lot of undead down there, but I'm not seeing anywhere near the number you guys told me about. Maybe one really big one and a few other smaller ones is more accurate. At most…10,000."

"Wow…"

I was thoroughly impressed that she could get a sense of their numbers from this height. I mean, I liked to think that I had pretty good vision and could generally make out small details, but figuring out what was going on in a city 2,000 meters below was another thing entirely.

Regardless, we had a far graver problem than my vision on our hands—that of the number of undead in the city.

The messenger had said that Larisa was under attack by an army of at least 200,000. If they weren't in the city below, that meant they'd already left, and the ones here were merely to prevent anyone from taking the city back.

Factoring in the number of days it must have taken the messenger to reach the margrave, and then for the margrave to make it to Nohzan, quite a bit of time must have passed since the city was first attacked.

It was possible that the undead army had moved on to Brahniey and were already there, but based on Goemon's observations in the Delfrent Kingdom, it didn't sound like they left immediately after crushing their objective.

The man-spiders leading the armies could move about as fast as a horse, but the general rank-and-file troops could only manage human speeds.

I felt certain that we still had at least some time left.

"Felfi Visrotte, would you mind letting me down for a moment? I'd like to draw the location."

I figured it couldn't hurt to make a sketch of Larisa in my teleportation diary, should a situation arise where I needed to get back here in a hurry.

"Sure thing, lemme find a place to land." Felfi Visrotte tilted her wings and dropped into a steep dive.

"Waaaaaaugh?!"

"Kyii!"

She jerked back suddenly, and a massive blast of air caused me to temporarily float up off of her back. I tried scrunching myself down as small as I could to hang on tight.

A moment later, I heard a loud crash and felt her whole body reverberate beneath me.

Venturing a glance over the side, I discovered that Felfi Visrotte had landed right on two man-spiders and was batting undead soldiers with her tail, deftly deflecting oncoming blows with its crystalline tip.

In a single, massive sweep of her tail, she wiped out a large group, like a god of death wielding a soul-reaping scythe.

"Now that's a stench that's hard to get out of your nose." She scowled at the stench of rotting flesh. Despite her initial attack, there were still quite a few undead left.

We'd landed a fair bit away from the entrance to Larisa, in what must have once been a field. As I dropped to the ground, I felt wheat stalks crunch beneath my feet. This year's harvest seemed like a lost cause. However, some fields seemed to have been spared, so if there were any survivors, at least they'd have something to eat.

I turned my attention to the city, a vast wasteland filled with dead and undead alike.

Aware of the pressure of time we were under, I pulled out my teleportation diary and tried to get a feel for my surroundings.

Before I could start, however, I caught sight of several undead soldiers and man-spiders closing in on me. I'd never get my sketch done if I had to keep fending them off, so I shot a pleading look up at the Dragon Lord.

"Sorry to bother you, but would you mind taking care of these pests while I finish my work?"

The large dragon propped herself up and puffed out her chest.

"Not a problem. I'll play around with 'em for a bit while you do your thing. Just call out to me when you're done, 'kay?"

She gave her wings a flap, sending up a whirlwind of dust, before launching off toward the oncoming enemy. The air snapped as she swung her tail around, like a bull-whip breaking the sound barrier.

In no time at all, the undead were lying in pieces, while what was left of the destroyed crops floated about like a golden snowstorm.

"Kyii! Kyiiiii!" Ponta mewed at me, as if prompting me to get back to work.

I hurriedly opened my teleportation diary and stared down at the empty page. If I didn't get this done soon, she might finish off the undead out here and move on to those inside the capital.

Since I didn't have much time, I just focused on one part of the city wall, sketching it as simply and as quickly as I could. I could fill in the details later.

"As long it's accurate enough to jog my memory, that should be enough."

I held the teleportation diary up and looked back and forth between the sketch and the wall a few times before giving a satisfied nod. It was a bit rough, but it captured all the unique details.

With that done, I put my supplies back into my bag and looked about until I spotted the Dragon Lord smashing undead like ants. I waved my arms as I called to her.

"Felfi Visrotte!"

Fortunately, she seemed to have excellent hearing, and she instantly turned her neck to look at me. With one final swipe of her tail to clear away the lingering undead soldiers, she darted through the air back to my side.

"Well, that was faster than I expected."

She narrowed her reptilian eyes, staring at the gates of the capital.

"Something wrong?"

"Kyii?"

Ponta and I looked at the Dragon Lord with concern, but she shook her head and turned her attention back to me.

"I sensed a large presence in the city earlier, but now it's gone."

I looked up at the battered walls, but try as I might, my senses were nowhere near as keen as Ariane and Chiyome's. I couldn't sense anything similar to what Felfi Visrotte was talking about.

She clearly wasn't talking about the man-spiders or undead. The only things I could think of were either the pontiff or one of his cardinals.

Being able to disappear all of a sudden also suggested that they were able to use teleportation magic like me, in which case it'd be impossible to follow them. We needed to focus on more pressing matters.

"I'm afraid the main undead army is likely marching on Brahniey as we speak. I'd like to try and track them down, if you'd be willing to help with that."

Our original plan had been to come out here and find a place to teleport troops to, then immediately head back to Saureah to notify Ariane. But if the undead army was already closing in on Brahniey, then figuring out their current location was of the utmost importance. Depending on where they were, it could change our plans entirely.

Fortunately, Felfi Visrotte agreed to my request without a second thought.

"I said I'd help, didn't I? So no need for you to make all these little requests. Just hop on my back and hold on tight!"

I adjusted the bag on my back, pulled Ponta close to my chest, and hopped onto Felfi Visrotte's back. She seemed to take this as the sign that I was ready and immediately rocketed into the sky.

"Thanks, I appreciate iiiiiiiiiiiiit!"

I squeezed my body against her back and held on. Ponta seemed to be having a grand time.

"Kyiiiiiii!"

Once we got up to altitude and the wind died down, Felfi Visrotte started moving through the air in slow circles. She glanced back at me to check where we were heading.

"Brahniey is off to the east, right?"

"That's correct."

She nodded and turned. "And we're off!"

She gave a powerful flap of her massive wings, causing the wavy violet patterns on the membranes to glow, before blasting off toward our objective.

Since I was taking the brunt of the wind, Ponta loved moving at such high speed.

"Kyii! Kyiiiii!"

I noticed that the wind around Ponta seemed to be weaker, probably thanks to its magic. It was pretty impressive. From what I'd heard, cottontail foxes often traveled on wind currents in large packs, so it only made sense that they would be able to strengthen or weaken such gusts.

I, for one, would have given anything for that kind of power while I fought not to be thrown to my doom.

Fortunately, it wasn't long until Felfi Visrotte slowed, and the buffeting wind calmed slightly. She called my attention to the scene below.

"Heya, Arc, look down."

I glanced over her side and swallowed hard. "That's... Wow."

The plains were covered with what looked like a black, undulating carpet moving east—the tightly packed undead soldiers.

They didn't move anything like the trained soldiers I'd encountered in the Holy East Revlon Empire's colony on the southern continent, but they were still progressing steadily, marching slowly but surely toward Brahniey and the Ruanne Forest.

"They're not far from Larisa, so we still have time until they arrive at their destination. But this definitely isn't a good sign."

Even Ponta watched the black blob with great interest. "Kyii!"

"If they were all clumped together, I could wipe 'em all out with a single strike. But they're too spread out right now. I'd need to chase a lot of 'em down."

Felfi Visrotte made no effort to conceal her annoyance. She turned to look at me, a scowl on her face.

"So, what're we gonna do, Arc?"

"Hmm..."

If hundreds of undead soldiers were packed tightly into a single formation, an area-of-effect spell should be able to wipe them out in one go. However, with them dotting the entire countryside like this, it would take several hundred of our biggest attacks to kill them all.

Felfi Visrotte and I could probably do it on our own, but we didn't have a lot of time to spare.

Sending the troops to Larisa was pointless now, so

we needed to find a second drop-off location. That left either the border of the margrave's territory, or the city of Brahniey itself.

However, there was a very real risk that the undead army would split off before reaching Brahniey and send half of their forces south as an advance strike on the village of Drant in the Ruanne Forest.

We needed to figure out a place to attack them before then. But where?

I thought back to the map I'd looked at earlier, trying to recall some sort of landmark.

"What about the Wiel River that runs along the border? They'll need to stop there and get organized, don't ya think?"

It was as if Felfi Visrotte could read my mind. I'd been thinking of the exact same place.

"Agreed. I think it'd be a good idea to set our teleportation spot at one of the forts on the border."

Margrave Brahniey had said that there were a series of forts east of the Wiel that had once belonged to the Nohzan Kingdom. They were from the days before his ancestors had taken possession of the land. He'd maintain them meticulously, and they were still fit for service.

Though technically just spaces to garrison the troops charged with maintaining the border, they served another important purpose—to keep an eye on the nobles as they traveled around the Salma Kingdom.

Before the forts were actually up and running, villages across Brahniey's domain had often been attacked by bandits. Ariane had been shocked to hear this, though King Asparuh had looked unsurprised. The margrave had to be constantly on alert for raids not only by outsiders, but also from his own countrymen.

In any case, I figured that one of the forts overlooking the Wiel would be a good place to start.

"Do you think you could fly past this group and let me off near the river? I'd like to set our new teleportation point there and then head back to Saureah."

Felfi Visrotte nodded. "All right. We're off again!"

She twisted her mammoth body around in mid-air and turned back east.

Fortunately, none of the undead soldiers marching along the plains seemed to take any notice of us as we flew above them at breakneck speed. Within a few moments, they were just a dark stain in the distance.

I had to squint in order to keep an eye on where we were going through the gusts of wind buffeting my body. Assuming Felfi Visrotte was flying at the same speed as when we'd left this morning, I could calculate how long we'd have until the undead army arrived at the Wiel.

I caught sight of a river up ahead, winding its way from north to south. That had to be it, with the peaks beyond being the Sobir mountain range.

Judging by the time it had taken us to pass over the undead army and get here, my best guess was that they'd only recently set out from Larisa. The road they'd be taking traveled mostly across flat plains, though there was a mountainous region where the road grew narrow and the soldiers would have to bunch up to pass through.

Figuring this would slow them down, I guessed that would give us two, maybe three days until they arrived at the Wiel.

I could see two forts, each surrounded by their own robust stone walls. These were heavily fortified locations from back in the days when the Nohzan Kingdom had needed to fend off their invading neighbors, though by garrisoning his own forces here, the margrave had done a good job cutting off most of the easy routes any roaming bandits could use to gain entry.

Next to the fort was a magnificent stone bridge that ran across the river. Though I couldn't tell how deep the water was, I was pretty sure the undead would need to cross that bridge in order to pass into Brahniey.

"Life certainly works in weird ways. What was once

used to harass belligerent nobles will now serve as a base of operations to mount our defense."

I was surprised at how things could take such a turn over time.

"Kyii!" Ponta seemed to be feeling much the same.

I truly had no idea if Ponta understood a word I said, but I gave its head a gentle rub all the same before instructing Felfi Visrotte to let me down near the fort.

Since leaving his lands for the Nohzan Kingdom, the margrave hadn't returned to his people, nor had he made any mention to those stationed at the outposts about the upcoming battle. The guards charged with watching the borders would know nothing about me, and the sight of an eighty-meter Dragon Lord would only alarm them.

On the other hand, my goal was to teleport the incoming armies as close to the fort as possible, so I couldn't be too far away if I wanted to get the details right.

They'd probably still notice us, but hopefully they'd assume this was just some sort of intimidation attempt. That should give me enough time to make a basic sketch for my teleportation diary. Then we could return to Saureah.

"Okay, hang on tight!"

The Dragon Lord dropped into another steep dive, heading straight toward the eastern bank of the Wiel.

The shoreline was completely bare, giving me a great view of the fort below and the soldiers running around in a panic at the sight of a dragon. The reaction was pretty much what I'd expected.

Even though we were trying to keep our distance, there was simply no way someone could ignore the impressive sight of a Dragon Lord.

Fortunately for me, the stone bridge spanning the river had a rather unique design, so I figured I'd be able to get off a quick sketch before we wore out our welcome.

"Once I'm done getting this down on paper, I'm going to use my teleportation magic to take us back to Saureah. Would you mind transforming into your humanoid form?"

Felfi Visrotte smiled and nodded.

Though it would have been possible for me to teleport her in her dragon form, it would require a lot of magic to do so—magic that I'd need to bring the margrave and about 5,000 soldiers here.

I slid off the Dragon Lord's back and started pulling out my supplies.

"Kyii!" Ponta hopped up onto my head while I focused my attention on the scene in front of me.

"We won't be staying long, Ponta. We'll be back in Saureah soon."

The Wiel River was at least 100 meters across, and probably double that in some places. The large banks on either side made it look even bigger.

However, that was where the good news ended. The river looked to be relatively shallow, with small eddies circling around rocks just under the surface. I doubted the man-spiders would have much difficulty making their way across.

I started drawing while Felfi Visrotte began her transformation.

Just as she was about to finish, I looked up and noticed several soldiers in the fort's watchtowers. They were pointing right at us and talking hurriedly among themselves.

A part of me felt a little bad that they'd have to explain to their superiors why they'd claimed to have seen a massive dragon when there was now nothing of the sort anywhere around.

"Kyii! Kyiiiii!"

Ponta patted my helmet, reminding me to focus on the task at hand. I turned my gaze away from the tower and began sketching again.

Once I had the general design down, I held my teleportation diary up and checked it against the actual bridge. Felfi Visrotte leaned over my shoulder for a closer look.

"Not bad, kid."

"Let's head back to Saureah."

I turned to Felfi Visrotte as I slid my teleportation diary back into my bag. She wore a faint grin on her face, as if remembering something from her distant past.

"Y'know, it's been quite a while since I've teleported anywhere."

Now that I thought about it, I remembered hearing that Evanjulin had also used teleportation magic. Maybe they'd traveled around together?

"Transport Gate!"

A magical rune spread out from beneath my feet until it was wide enough to encompass Felfi Visrotte as well. She watched with great interest.

I focused my mind on the courtyard in front of the palace in Saureah, which we'd left mere hours ago. The world went dark, and an instant later, we were back in Nohzan.

Felfi Visrotte stretched out her arms and nodded approvingly. "That's a pretty useful technique."

"It's thanks to your incredible speed that we were able to return here in less than half a day."

Considering she'd probably never let people ride her before, I felt it only proper to thank her for all she'd done.

"You've really got your act together, kid. Nothing like Eva." She tilted her head to the side and gazed at me with great interest. "So, what's next?"

She smiled, and began wagging her long, dagger-tipped tail.

"Well, I suppose we'd better share what we've learned."

After turning to face the castle, I pulled Ponta close and started walking.

"Kyii! Kyiiiii!"

We gathered with Ariane, Chiyome, Goemon, and the other leaders in a room deep within the castle to discuss the next phase of our fight against the Holy Hilk Kingdom's assault.

Everyone crowded around close to me and Felfi Visrotte, their eyes fixed on the map.

The white tokens sat exactly where we'd left them the night before. I took one of the black tokens and moved it from Larisa, in the Salma Kingdom, to a spot farther east.

A look of shock overcame the margrave as his eyes followed the token. "Wait, you mean to say they've already begun their advance?!"

"That's correct. We only found a few undead in Larisa, just enough to maintain control over the region, while the rest of the army moved east toward Brahniey."

Felfi Visrotte tapped the black token with her fingertip.

"We coulda wiped 'em out right then and there if they'd marched in columns like you humans, but no luck."

King Asparuh, Prince Sekt, and Margrave Brahniey—the human representatives in this alliance—frowned. Princess Riel looked puzzled at their shared reaction and turned to her father.

"If Felfi Visrotte is as powerful as everyone says, then we've got nothing to worry about if the undead attack us. So why are you scowling like that, Father?"

King Asparuh shifted uncomfortably under his daughter's intense gaze and cleared his throat.

Margrave Brahniey looked straight at me. "How long do we have until they reach Brahniey? I don't need an exact hour, just an estimate." The margrave's eyes pleaded with me. He was clearly clinging to the hope that there was still time.

"At my best guess, I'd say two days. Three, tops."

He groaned at this, deep wrinkles forming in his forehead. "That's much faster than I would have expected."

Dillan, also scowling down at the map, offered some clarification on how they could cover so much ground.

"Unlike the living, the undead need not eat nor rest, so they can focus entirely on moving. Judging by the lay of the land, it would take less than four days to cover that distance."

He was right, of course. The undead weren't burdened with the obligation to waste time on feeding and resting their soldiers.

As an added bonus, this meant that they didn't need to deal with carts or the animals that drew them. They were only limited by the speed at which a person could march under the full weight of gear.

These were, in a sense, the ultimate soldiers. They could march twenty-four hours a day and still fight once they reached their destination. Plus, they were already dead, so they had no fear of death in battle.

While I might look like one of them, I still enjoyed eating, sleeping, and even a nice bath. We were, in these respects, fundamentally different.

Felfi Visrotte picked up one of the white tokens, moving it toward the Wiel River.

"We've decided to make our stand here, at the Wiel, since they'll need to stop there. We'll take care of as many as we can and leave the rest to you. Think you can handle that?"

King Asparuh and Margrave Brahniey looked worried

at this rather brazen plan, while Fangas and Dillan nodded confidently.

Fangas even smiled. "I've been looking forward to the day when I could finally see the great Dragon Lord in battle."

This seemed to reassure Asparuh and Brahniey, and they nodded their assent.

Here, in the presence of a Dragon Lord who spoke of facing off against 200,000 undead as if it were nothing and a dark elf elder who laughed at the thought of the upcoming battle, it was clear the humans were way out of their league.

All they'd have to do was take care of any survivors that made it past Felfi Visrotte's attack.

Though I would have loved to see that battle unfold, it was quickly becoming clear that she would handle the Salma front while I held off the assault in the Delfrent Kingdom.

Dillan laid out his plan. "All right, we'll place around 1,000 soldiers in the two forts on the Wiel River and defend from there."

With no objections, it seemed that the matter was settled.

Dillan picked up two white tokens and placed them next to the Wiel.

"We don't have a lot of time to prepare. On the Salma front, Fangas will command the elven soldiers and Prince Sekt will lead his. Arc, I'd like you to take care of teleportation."

He picked up two more white tokens and set one down on a forest and another on a town.

"After the troops have been moved to their new location, I'd like the margrave to return to Brahniey to muster his troops. Fangas will head to Drant in the Ruanne Forest to bring together the other elven soldiers who've agreed to join us."

He turned back to me.

"Once you're done preparing the Salma front, Arc, I want you to head to Delfrent so we can get our troops out there as soon as possible. We'll be relying on you and Villiers Fim for this fight, with some support from the Jinshin clan and soldiers from Canada."

I held Dillan's gaze as I voiced my concern. "If Felfi Visrotte will be stationed on the border with the Salma Kingdom, then it will take me quite some time to reach Lione in the Delfrent Kingdom."

Now that we knew the undead were moving far faster than we'd originally assumed, everything on the Delfrent front had changed as well. Sure, Goemon and his comrades had observed the undead armies still lurking around the capital, but much time had passed since then. The situation could have easily changed.

Since there was no easy way to send information across long distances in this world, other than my teleportation magic or a Dragon Lord, there was an added pressure of simply not knowing exactly where the undead were or what they were doing.

They'd already toppled both the Delfrent and Salma kingdoms with relative ease, after all.

Having lived my entire life in the modern world, where we had the advantage of quick transport and information exchange, I felt completely out of my element here.

I was trying to say that if we hoped to strike a definitive blow against the undead, then I would need to borrow Felfi Visrotte for a little while longer. However, she quickly offered up a different plan.

"I don't see the problem here. I brought another Dragon Lord along with me, didn't I? If I ask him, there's no way he'll say no."

Her mouth curled up into another one of her trademark grins.

Just thinking about riding on Villiers Fim reminded me of our first encounter, when I'd kicked him right in the back. I let out a quiet laugh at this interesting turn of events.

To the west of Brahniey, the Wiel River flowed out of the Sobir Mountains and ran south, creating a natural border with the rest of the Salma Kingdom.

An imposing stone bridge spanning the river served as a critical road that connected Brahniey's domain with the capital of Larisa. This was flanked by large forts, originally built by the Nohzan Kingdom, where soldiers were garrisoned to watch over the roads and all who crossed the bridge.

These refurbished forts were typically quite large compared to the number of soldiers stationed within them, but their tranquil atmosphere was disrupted as hundreds of new soldiers descended upon them with a certain excited fervor.

In addition to the guards who maintained posts here, there were now soldiers from Brahniey, the Rhoden Kingdom, and even the elven realms roaming about.

The elven soldiers from the Great Canada Forest had been joined by elves from the village of Drant in the Ruanne Forest, led by village elders Iwahld and Serge.

Many of the humans stationed here had never seen an elf before and couldn't help but stare, as if they were some great novelty.

But it wasn't only their elongated ears that drew the human's attention. It was also the fact that the elven ranks were filled with women, something practically unheard of in the male-dominated human military. This actually helped them cope with the anxiety of standing on the front lines of a battle against the undead, a battle for their very survival.

One of the soldiers leaned over and whispered to his comrades. "Y'say that the purple lady's a dark elf? Man, you see the way her chest bounces when she walks? I gotta admit, she really does perk things up around here."

Several soldiers slapped the man on his back.

"I know you're desperate, but you best keep yer little buddy in your pants there, my friend. Man or woman, the elves are ferocious fighters. I already saw some drunk idiot come on a little too strong with one of the elven women. She worked him over so bad that they had to send him to a medic."

The man shrugged dismissively. "Don't lump me in with that idiot! I wouldn't dare try something like that."

Everyone was already experiencing a mixture of excitement over the upcoming battle and a severe case of nerves at the thought of facing a massive army of the undead. No matter how attractive someone might be, they still had a job to focus on. The people gathered here were the best their respective countries had to offer, and with that came a certain sense of duty. They all knew too well that they were fighting for the survival of their species.

Humans, elves, and even mountain people were all here to face a common foe. They'd been warned by their commanders not to do anything that would disturb the peace. But even though no one would dare say it out loud, it was clear that the humans felt uncomfortable having all these non-humans around.

Suddenly waking up to thousands of soldiers appearing out of nowhere, not to mention seeing elves, a species many had only heard about in fairytales, was a shock in its own right. Even more shocking was the sheer power on parade before their very eyes. The elven forces were superior in every way to anything the humans could offer. If the elves chose not to cooperate in the coming battle, the humans were pretty much done for.

As such, the humans treated them with the utmost respect. Their commanders would frequently go around "inspecting" the elven encampments so that they could offer praise on everything the elves had. Not a single human dared voice their annoyance at this preferential treatment. And when the large dragon landed in the courtyard, that pretty much put an end to even the thought of squabbling.

Until recently, the Dragon Lord known as Felfi Visrotte had been nothing but a legend, the topic of many songs and poems. No one had believed that such a magnificent creature actually existed until they witnessed her soaring high in the sky on her violet-tinted wings.

At an impressive eighty meters long, the sight of her was so awe-inspiring that no one dared to step out of line, regardless of their rank or how full of bravado they usually were.

The Dragon Lord brought power beyond comprehension. One would have to be exceedingly dense to take a hard stance against the elves now, especially knowing that they could call upon the impressive might of a Dragon Lord if needed.

This made many human soldiers question whether their presence was even necessary. However, this entire battle was based on the idea of a unified front. If that cooperative spirit were lost, the dignity of the human species would be lost along with it. Each and every soldier here, from the untestedy novice to grizzled veteran, knew that much.

Fortunately, the troops' morale was bolstered by the fact that they had powerful allies. Even that, however, was nothing compared to the revelation that the undead army they were about to face was commanded by the Holy Hilk Kingdom. They were barely able to contain their surprise upon hearing these words.

Recalling this, one of the soldiers who'd been listening to the previous exchange brought the subject back up. The disbelief was still evident on his face.

"D'ya think the Holy Hilk Kingdom is really using some kinda dark magic to control all these undead like they say?"

The other soldiers stopped cleaning their weapons for a moment and exchanged glances. There were some who didn't—couldn't—believe these claims, while other reactions ranged from confusion to disillusionment with the church.

The Holy Hilk Kingdom was the de facto head of the Hilk religion, the most prominent religion on the northern continent. For practitioners of the faith, it was hard to overcome their long-held belief that the Holy Hilk Kingdom was beyond reproach.

According to King Asparuh and Margrave Wendly, the Holy Hilk Kingdom had used dark magic to create an army of the undead and was now crushing their neighboring kingdoms. While no one went so far as to say that their leaders were telling lies, it was difficult to reconcile these statements with their idea of the church. It was like being stuck between a rock and a hard place.

The only ones who didn't seem particularly troubled by this declaration were the soldiers from the Rhoden Kingdom, where the majority held their country in higher regard than the church's teachings.

But for the soldiers of Brahniey, who'd been raised from childhood to believe that the church's teachings were universally true, the idea of having to change their entire worldview shook them to their very core. Despite their uncertainty, however, they all had unwavering faith in the margrave. Such was the influence he wielded.

"Y'know, I got a buddy who traveled with the margrave to the Nohzan Kingdom. According to him, some of the locals were saying that when the Hilk cardinal faced off against the elves, he turned into a giant monster."

The soldiers leaned close, intrigued by this bit of information, and urged him to continue. The man smiled at his enraptured comrades.

"In fact, they say that all the Hilk cardinals are monsters. The whole reason the Hilk even preached about kicking around the elves and beast people was because they're the only ones who can tell the cardinals aren't human."

This was met with several suspicious glares.

The Holy Hilk Kingdom being behind this whole ordeal was hard enough to believe. The idea that their ranks were made up of monsters was downright outrageous.

Moreover, it meant that the soldiers themselves were complicit in the Hilk plot by following the teachings that had been ingrained in them since birth.

Whether or not the man's story was true, the soldiers around him agreed that something significant must have happened in order to bring the species of the world together.

The soldiers hadn't had nearly enough time to come to terms with the tempest of emotions racing through them when the situation took a sudden turn for the worse.

Every day, the Dragon Lord would fly off toward Larisa and report back on what she'd found. Today was no different. The guards on watch spotted her as expected.

She flew straight over the fort and landed in a large clearing nearby to describe her findings. A short time later, messengers were dispatched to notify the troops to prepare for an attack.

The soldiers, who just moments before had been chattering like schoolchildren, immediately made their way toward the fort's outer wall to get a look at who they'd be up against. They squinted at the far bank of the Wiel.

A low, gray fog hung in the air, limiting visibility. However, they could just make out a faint, black blob spreading across the horizon. They swallowed hard as the blob began taking shape.

As this indistinct darkness crested the hill on the other side of the river, it spread out even more, continuing its slow march toward the Wiel.

The undead didn't move like any army these soldiers had seen before. It was like they all happened to be moving east toward Brahniey together in a large mass. There was something about the sight that sent chills up the spines of all who watched.

From a distance, the undead looked like infantry in dull armor, moving about in small squads. There were so many of them that they were impossible to count. The knowledge that these were no mere foot soldiers made the humans' skin crawl.

Among the squads were other bizarre creatures that clearly weren't human. The soldiers let out quiet gasps of horror as these freaks of nature took shape.

One of them muttered his thoughts aloud to no one in particular. "It's like the entire continent is covered in monsters..."

The feeling was mutual among the soldiers watching this scene unfold.

The bizarre creatures stood much taller than the undead around them. They seemed to be made of the lower half of a spider, while their upper body consisted of two human torsos melded together, each sporting two arms and wielding a variety of weapons.

Neither human nor beast, these abominations were like nothing the soldiers had ever seen. Worse, they seemed to be leading the squads around them as they prepared to cross the Wiel.

The forts began ringing their alarm bells to notify all soldiers in the vicinity that the undead army was approaching.

Up in one of the fort's towers, Margrave Brahniey and Fangas stood watch.

The margrave groaned. "Even knowing this was coming, I still can't believe it. Hearing is one thing. Seeing such an army with my own eyes is another thing entirely."

When the messenger from Salma had first shown up with a report on what had happened in the capital, the margrave had understood on an intellectual level just how grave things were. That's why he'd immediately headed for the Nohzan Kingdom to seek help.

While there, by sheer luck, he was able to get his request out to the elves, beast people, and even the Rhoden Kingdom, and muster a force far greater than he could have ever hoped for.

He glared across the Wiel at the slowly approaching undead.

If they failed to hold the line, then everyone within his domain was doomed. He felt his muscles tense under the burden of that responsibility.

At his side, Fangas clapped Margrave Brahniey on the shoulder and smiled. "You look tense, Wendly. Don't forget, we have Felfi Visrotte on our side. So long as we stick to the plan, there's nothing to worry about."

Fangas unclasped the heavy war hammer from his back and swung it effortlessly into the stone tiling beneath their feet. A dull thud reverberated through the room.

"Warriors of Canada, heed my call!"

His voice boomed out from the tower.

"Archers, launch a barrage of arrows to keep them in place! Felfi Visrotte will strike when the time is right! Now, show 'em what we're made of!!!"

The elven soldiers let out a thunderous roar and lifted their weapons skyward. Brightly colored flags were raised from the tops of the watchtowers surrounding the fort, billowing in the strong breeze off the river. The second fort soon followed suit with their own flags.

The signal given, the archers hurried to their positions and took aim.

On the far bank of the Wiel, the front of the undead

army had just reached the water's edge and were preparing to ford the river. Though they were undead, they were still limited to crossing where the water was shallow enough and they could maintain their footing. This caused the squads to cluster together.

The man-spiders rushed ahead, as if impatient to lead the charge, tossing their own soldiers out of the way like rag dolls to be dragged under by the powerful current.

The undead soldiers continued their march forward, even as they began dropping, one after the next, into the river's depths.

Margrave Brahniey stared in astonishment. "Just what in the hell..."

He wasn't the only one at a loss for words. Soldiers all around the perimeter watched in surprise.

The elves' expertly aimed arrows were finding their marks and thinning the ranks of the undead.

While the fort was somewhat close to the river, there were still a good 500 meters between the archers and their targets. Even with the added difficulty of the breeze off the water, the elves were still able to find their marks. This kind of archery was leaps beyond what the best humans could do. Their arrows seemed almost self-propelled, hitting their targets even when the undead attempted to dodge.

The aerial onslaught wasn't limited to the infantry

either. Even the musclebound man-spiders took their share of casualties from the barrage, despite their armor.

The arrows exploded the moment they pierced the man-spiders' flesh, sending limbs in every direction. Once a man-spider was incapacitated, the archers would follow up with another two or three arrows until it was nothing but a lump of meat.

Margrave Brahniey watched with great interest as the elves showed off their marksmanship. Looking closer, he noticed that the archers were chanting an incantation before launching each arrow. They were using magic to power each shot.

Alas, no matter how good their archers might be, the casualties they inflicted were little more than a drop in the bucket against the invading army. Between the two forts, nearly 1,000 elven soldiers fired volley after volley, but it just wasn't enough to make a significant impact against the army of 200,000 undead.

It wasn't all for naught, however, as it had the effect of putting the enemy on the defensive and caused the man-spiders to order a halt. Slowly but surely, the undead fell back and reassembled on the far shore of the river. It looked as if their plan now was to rush ahead all at once, rather than sending small squads, in order to limit the effect of the arrow barrage.

The fact that they could make such a tactical move was all the proof the humans and elves needed that these were no normal, mindless undead. Someone was clearly commanding these forces.

Fangas whistled at the peculiar sight. "Knowing something logically and seeing it for yourself are completely different, eh, Wendly? I doubt I'd have believed it had I not witnessed it with my own eyes."

Brahniey nodded. Fortunately, even this had been accounted for in their plan.

The two men watched as the undead bunched up on the far shore. Excitement welled within them as they anticipated what would happen next. It was only a matter of time.

Fangas looked up at the wispy clouds. "Any second now..."

A moment later, he spotted Felfi Visrotte floating high above the battlefield, flapping her wings and building up magic as she waited for the perfect moment.

Once she was ready, a powerful ball of magic as bright as the sun appeared above her head, glowing white-hot. It grew bigger and bigger as she pumped more energy into it.

The undead began their second rush across the Wiel, moving forward in an endless stream through the barrage of elven arrows. When one fell, another stepped up to take its place.

The archers shivered, their brows wrinkling as the arrows seemed to have less and less effect.

Then, everything changed.

The Dragon Lord grabbed the glowing object above her head and hurled it down at the undead army below. Fangas gave the signal, and the fort's alarm bells immediately began ringing in a slow, controlled rhythm.

Squad leaders, who'd been briefed on what to do once they heard this bell, began shouting orders for their troops to get into defensive positions.

"Lower your weapons and get down! Everyone, behind the wall!"

Margrave Brahniey and his aides ducked below the window in their small watchtower while Fangas continued standing in the center of the room. He gave a wide, toothy grin as the ball of light descended silently in front of them.

The whole world went white.

BAFOOOOOOOOOOOOOOM!!!

The thundering explosion was followed by an equally powerful pressure wave that caused the very earth to groan as the fort's foundation strained. A moment later, soldiers' fearful cries reached the margrave's ears.

A shower of pebbles and fist-sized rocks ruthlessly pelted the hunkering soldiers, followed by a deluge of water that turned the dust covering their bodies into mud.

Margrave Brahniey's ears were still ringing as he pulled himself to his feet. He had to yell to the soldiers next to him just to be understood.

Though everyone knew to expect a powerful magical attack, none of them had experienced anything quite like this before. It defied all expectations.

In stark contrast with the confused yelling coming from the humans, the elven soldiers pumped their fists excitedly and cheered.

Even Fangas, who'd somehow managed to remain standing, was laughing raucously.

Once the soldiers had composed themselves, they readjusted their gear and ventured a look over the wall at the massive dust cloud beyond. What they saw left them speechless.

A massive crater sat in the middle of the river, slowly filling with water. In time, there would be a new lake, interrupting the Wiel's meandering journey.

Beyond the river, the undead appeared to have been reduced by at least half their original strength, thanks to the Dragon Lord's powerful blast.

The margrave could barely comprehend the sight in front of him.

The stone bridge that had once taken thousands of travelers over the river was now a pile of rubble. The only hints that it had ever existed were the sturdy foundations connected to the shore.

In contrast to the shocked silence of everyone else around the fort, Fangas didn't show a hint of surprise at the results of the attack. He rested his mammoth hammer on his shoulder as he surveyed the scene.

"You got 'em, Felfi! Knocked 'em flat on their asses with just one blow! The rest should be easy pickings."

Since the enemy was incapable of feeling fear—or any emotion at all, for that matter—they simply continued their march down the hill and through the devastation. With their numbers greatly reduced, the sight of the marching undead was now more bewildering than intimidating. If anything, it was a somewhat pitiful sight.

Fangas lifted his war hammer into the air and shouted for all the soldiers to hear.

"It's about time we return these dead bodies to the earth and free their spirits once and for all! This world has no place for the dead!"

The soldiers, human and elf alike, raised their weapons as well and cheered.

"The great Dragon Lord has tipped the scales in our favor!" Fangas continued. "But that doesn't mean we can let our guard down just yet! I want you to chase down and kill every last one of these soldiers until peace once again returns to these lands! Soldiers of Canada, focus on the spider monsters! The rest of you, take to the tree line and rout the enemy!"

Even with a majority of the invaders killed, there were still tens of thousands of undead to contend with. This was no time to relax.

After using all her power on that one attack, Felfi Visrotte would have to sit out the rest of the battle. However, she'd managed to completely turn the tide of battle and give the mud-covered soldiers a chance at winning the unwinnable.

The elven archers standing watch began taking aim at the man-spiders, while the others split into squads and rushed out of the fort to begin the grueling task of close-quarters combat.

While the elves were accustomed to operating in small groups and adjusting tactics on the fly, the humans struggled with this type of combat. The soldiers of Brahniey watched as the elves engaged the enemy and waited passively for their own orders.

Margrave Brahniey began barking commands. "Execute the plan like we discussed! I want the cavalry out first to take care of the armored soldiers. Leave the spider monsters to the elves! Watch their backs and provide whatever support you can! Those in the fort, prepare stones to drop on anything that tries to penetrate these walls!"

The soldiers rushed to their stations. Meanwhile, Sekt and the knights of the Rhoden Kingdom were already flying out the front gate.

His mounted soldiers, numbering nearly 1,000 strong, rode in one long line and tore straight into the oncoming undead. Those who happened near man-spiders thrust their long spears into the monsters as they passed. It was like watching a snake slither across the battlefield.

At the head of this impressive charge was Prince Sekt himself, with several of his personal guards following close behind.

Margrave Brahniey watched, impressed, and let out a sigh of longing as he looked down at his wrinkled hands.

"Ah, the vigor of youth. Alas, my days of leading from the front lines are long behind me."

Brahniey thought of his secretary and his beloved family back home.

While he'd found himself completely bewildered at the terrifying sight of the enemy, Prince Sekt had carried his knights straight into battle without a second thought. That was the kind of leadership they needed right now.

A smile spread across Brahniey's face as he recalled the old days when he, too, had led the charge with sword held high. It might pain him to admit it, but those days had passed.

Shaking his head, he looked over to Fangas, a man who almost certainly understood the ache of being away from the battlefield.

But the high elder was nowhere to be seen. After checking the watchtower, Brahniey finally gave up and looked out the window again to check on the battle. He spotted an old man standing, eyes closed, directly in Prince Sekt's path.

Prince Sekt also took notice of the figure. Dressed in elaborate robes, the old man easily stood out from all the other undead soldiers.

Though dressed like a priest, the old man was a hulking figure covered in muscles. Despite his wrinkled brow and wispy white hair, he looked like he could give even Fangas a run for his money.

The most noteworthy thing about the old man, however, was the massive sword he wore on his back. It was nearly as long as he was tall.

He stood completely still on the frenzied battlefield, though his face trembled with barely contained rage, evident even though his eyes were closed. A cold sweat broke out on the back of Sekt's neck as a deep foreboding overtook him.

"Well, well! I hope you're proud of yourselves! You will all suffer heinous deaths for causing me to lose His Holiness's troops!"

The man's voice boomed, his words somehow rising above the thundering hooves to reach everyone on the battlefield. Prince Sekt felt the sinister sound vibrate through his body.

The old man's torso twitched, and his muscles began growing even larger, his clothes tearing at the seams. Faces with bloodred eyes grew from his shoulders. He reached back and unsheathed his sword, holding it at the ready.

Prince Sekt ordered his men to split around the old man, creating two large snakes that writhed across the battlefield.

The old man lunged, swinging his massive sword straight toward the prince.

At the front of the formation, Sekt was far closer to the man than he would have liked. He dug his heels into his horse's sides to urge it out of the way.

A moment later, he was thrown from the saddle.

"Nngh?! Gwwaaaaugh!"

Sekt landed on his back with a heavy thud, all of the air knocked out of his lungs. A dull pain began spreading throughout his body. He caught sight of what had once been his horse, toppled onto its side, blood gushing out onto the ground. Had he paused just a moment longer, he would have met the same fate.

He looked up to see the old man advancing on him, ignoring the rest of the Rhoden army.

"Swordplay really isn't my specialty, y'know. But here goes."

Prince Sekt lurched to his feet, dragging his sleeve across his face to clear the blood from his mouth. He drew his elegantly decorated blade.

Though both of his legs seemed to be working fine, the same could only be said for one of his arms. The pain in his chest was so intense that he could barely breathe.

If the old man launched another strike, Sekt knew he'd meet the same fate as his horse. Yet he still managed to summon a smile.

The old man's mouth—now a long, monstrous gash—contorted at the prince's defiance. He swung his sword high above his head, the sky rumbling in response.

"You dare raise your sword against me, you disgusting little wretch?"

He spat the words as he swung his sword down toward the injured prince. Sekt brought up his own blade in a feeble attempt to parry.

Before the old man could land his blow, however, two Rhoden knights came rushing in on horseback, aiming their spears at the monster.

"Prince Sekt, get out of here!"

"Leave him to us!"

The old man changed the direction of his attack, his blade effortlessly cleaving the men in two, sending blood and organs splattering across the battlefield. All Prince Sekt could do was gape at the loss of his soldiers.

The bloodred eyes on the faces sticking out of the man's body snapped open, fixated on something rushing in from behind.

Sekt only noticed the newcomer when they landed on the ground in front of him, their war hammer slamming into the ground with explosive force.

"Seems like you managed to find the leader of these monsters, huh, kid?"

The muscles bulging under Fangas's amethyst skin glistened in the sunlight as he fixed his golden eyes on the old man in front of him. His whole body was tense, ready for a fight.

The old man's forehead creased at the dark elf's unwelcomed interference.

"You dare call His Holiness's followers monsters? That's rich, coming from a long-eared lizard descendant.

I suppose I should be impressed that you let the humans take the brunt of the assault though."

The old man took the hilt of his sword in both hands and pointed it at Fangas.

"I, Cardinal Augrent Iyla Patientia, will rid this world of your filthy kind. You should be grateful for His Holiness's benevolence."

Before he'd even finished speaking, Cardinal Augrent swung his sword at the high elder. Fangas deflected the blade with his war hammer and lunged for the cardinal's stomach.

The war hammer connected with an awful clang, knocking the cardinal back, though he didn't seem to suffer any sort of injury. On the contrary, this only enraged Cardinal Augrent further.

Fangas hefted his hammer, searching for an explanation as to why his attack hadn't done more damage. It was a solid hit, and he knew it.

"Cardinal, you say? So, the Holy Hilk Kingdom really is run by monsters."

The truth strained credulity. Between his ability to wield such a massive sword and the faces protruding from his skin, this musclebound abomination now bore only a passing resemblance to a human.

Despite his long life and vast experience, Fangas had never encountered a creature so wholly consumed by the contamination of death. He also knew that allowing such a creature to continue existing would be harmful for humans and elves alike.

Fangas would destroy the cardinal here and how.

He lowered his war hammer and lunged, this time swinging toward the cardinal's torso in an upward slash. However, Augrent caught the blow with his sword and knocked the dark elf back.

The two men exchanged blows, the air itself echoing sympathetically with each clash. The sheer strength brought to bear here was far beyond what most humans could ever hope to achieve.

Knowing that he would be of little use in this battle, Prince Sekt allowed two of his soldiers to carry him away. Even as he retreated, however, he couldn't tear his eyes off the fight.

Cardinal Augrent only grew angrier as the battle raged, becoming more reckless in his attacks.

"I'll rip you apart, you insolent barbarian!"

Fangas deflected another blow, and Augrent lifted his blade high over his head. Four sharpened tentacles tore out of the cardinal's body and shot toward the dark elf.

Fangas narrowly managed to dodge this unexpected attack, though he opened himself up to Augrent's blade in the process.

"Looks like we're a match in close quarters combat."

The dark elf didn't appear too concerned. In fact, he seemed to be enjoying himself.

"Piercing Earth Fang!" Fangas summoned his spirit energy and launched an attack of his own.

Gigantic spears of stone jutted out of the ground and shot straight toward the cardinal's back. Augrent's bloodred eyes went wide in surprise as the stone pierced his body and jutted out of his stomach.

He shot a hate-filled look in Fangas's direction.

"Ah, yes. I've heard your kind are known for using spirit magic. Alas, it will take a lot more than that to do me in." A sly grin crept across the cardinal's face.

Since the spears piercing Augrent's stomach clearly hadn't made much of an impact, Fangas launched another spirit magic attack.

"Great earth, heed my call! Use thy power to consume and punish our enemies!"

Jagged rocks burst forth in a circle around Augrent's feet and stabbed into him. The cardinal hung there, skewered in place.

"Grooooooooaaaaaawwwwl!"

Augrent thrashed about in an attempt to break free of the rocks pinning him in place.

Fangas hefted his war hammer and swung it with all

his might, connecting with the cardinal's chin and twisting his head back at an unnatural angle.

"You...f-f-filthy heathen!"

Any normal living being would certainly have been dead at this point, but somehow the cardinal continued to live, radiating hatred.

But this was of little concern to Fangas, who merely scowled in annoyance.

"You sure are a durable one, aren't you? I guess you don't plan on going down easy. But I'm going to put an end to you once and for all."

He gripped his war hammer in both hands and closed his eyes.

"Pull this bringer of death deep into the bowels of the earth to embrace his eternal slumber!"

Fangas's forehead creases deepened as he chanted, focusing all of his energy on this final attack. Augrent writhed and screamed in the face of such powerful spirit magic. He lost control over all the souls he'd consumed over the years as they ripped free from his body.

Earth and stone rose around Fangas and formed a gigantic boulder above Augrent's head. Light poured out from within, each ray that struck the cardinal's body causing him to thrash even harder. His eyes remained fixed on Fangas.

Augrent opened his mouth, as if to say something, but before he could speak, the gigantic mass of stone plummeted to the ground, smashing through the cardinal's body in the process.

Fangas smirked at the sight of the immense boulder sticking out of the earth.

"Such a beautiful grave. A shame it has to be wasted on the likes of you. I hope you appreciate it."

He then glanced around the battlefield to see how the rest of the fight was shaping up.

Felfi Visrotte was now on the ground, using her long tail and its razor-sharp tip to chop down legions of undead, while Prince Sekt's Rhoden knights, the elven squads, and the human foot soldiers were all wrapping up their own battles.

Fangas looked down at his war hammer.

"Sorry, old friend. Looks like you didn't get a chance to show off what you can do."

He let out a sigh and turned his gaze back to the battles raging around him, searching for an enemy.

"Looks like everyone pretty much has it handled. Now our fate is in your hands."

Fangas turned north, facing the Sobir Mountains and the Delfrent Kingdom. Ariane and Arc were heading there now.

Lione, the capital of the Delfrent Kingdom, stood out amid the vast plains. Smoke hung low over the city.

Chiyome watched intently, the ears atop her head twitching as she wrinkled her nose. "The stench of death emanates from the city. I can smell it from here."

The other Jinshin clan members sitting behind her made similar faces.

"I'd be surprised if anyone's still alive down there. The city is practically consumed by the contamination. I've never seen anything like it."

Ariane crossed her arms at Chiyome's dark words.

A warm gust of wind blew past us, throwing Ariane's snow-white hair all over the place. She scowled and shook her head, as if this would turn away the wind.

Dillan, leader of the forces on the Delfrent front, spoke up. "Now that everything's in place, I think it's time we put our plan into motion."

We were stationed just outside the vast forest that ran along the base of the mountains to the southwest of Lione.

Situated at the border separating the Holy Hilk Kingdom from the Delfrent Kingdom, this would normally be a terrible location to station an army, due to the risk of a pincer attack. But under the current circumstances, it was the ideal spot to watch our enemy's movements and launch a strike.

Thanks to Goemon's report, we were able to estimate just how far the enemy was scouting, and from what directions they were preparing to meet an attack. They'd neglected to consider an attack from the forest.

While the elves and the Jinshin clan were particularly gifted in the art of war, it was hard to imagine that our combined force of 5,000 could stand any significant chance against the 100,000 troops within the city. Hit-and-run tactics wouldn't have an impact.

To improve our odds, we'd taken advantage of the elves' spirit magic to build a series of ditches, berms, and defensive barriers around our position. Through these would likely prove ineffective against the highly mobile man-spiders, they should at least slow the undead foot soldiers.

The fact that we'd been able to get so much done in such a short period spoke to the elves' and Jinshin clan's skills.

A voice called out to Dillan from deep within the forest. "Is it time for me to start?"

A four-meter-tall humanoid figure with the head of a dragon stepped from the trees. It was Villiers Fim, waiting patiently for his moment in the battle.

Though nowhere near as large as Felfi Visrotte, Villiers Fim was still an impressive thirty meters long in his Dragon Lord form.

I'd originally expected him to balk at the request to join our fight, but much to my surprise, he'd responded with an eager smile. I figured this was largely due to his respect for Felfi Visrotte.

"I guess I'll be joining you."

Finished with my tree felling duties, I hefted my Holy Thunder Sword of Caladbolg and shot a sidelong glance at Ariane and Chiyome.

The four of us would be heading out to Lione where the undead had dug themselves in, to try and draw them out.

"Kyii!"

"Are you sure you want to come, Ponta? It's gonna be dangerous."

"Kyii!"

Apparently, Ponta's mind was set. That made us a party of five, then.

My gear consisted of the Holy Thunder Sword of Caladbolg and the Holy Shield of Teutates, as well as a waterskin full of spring water, just in case I needed it.

That should be more than enough to see the battle through, even if things got ugly.

By the time Ariane and Chiyome finished looking over their own gear, Villiers Fim had transformed back into his Dragon Lord form. Covered entirely in blue scales, he had four long, black horns jutting from his head, and four large wings extending from his back.

He would serve as the foundation for our assault, using his devastating area-of-effect attacks. Of course, I could also use my Paladin abilities as I had back in Saureah, but I wanted to avoid that, if possible.

"If you're ready, then let's get going."

Villiers Fim began flapping his wings, kicking up a powerful blast of wind as he lifted his giant body off the ground.

No matter how many times I witnessed this, it still amazed me to see these immense creatures airborne.

I reached up and grabbed onto one of Villiers Fim's hind legs, with Ponta wrapped tightly around my neck. Ariane, taken by surprise at our haphazard manner of climbing aboard, quickly grabbed on as well. Last was Chiyome, who effortlessly grabbed the leg opposite ours.

Once we were all on, Villiers Fim headed toward Lione. He was flying so low that I could watch the earth pass below me, making me feel both exhilarated and light-headed with the thrill of how fast we were going.

I'd always been a bit of an adrenaline junkie, but not

everyone shared my excitement. Ariane's face was turning increasingly pale.

"You're going too faaaaaaaaaaaaaaaast!"

She clung to the Dragon Lord and kicked her legs desperately to find purchase. It was rare to see Ariane so terrified, or hear her scream like that.

Chiyome, on the other hand, was completely unreadable. Her tail was stiff, and she had a tense expression on her face, but I had no idea what she was thinking.

"Kyii! Kyiiiii!"

Much like when we'd ridden on Felfi Visrotte's back, Ponta was simply having a great time.

As for why this trip was so much more heart-racing than the last, it was because Villiers Fim didn't like the idea of people riding on his back. But riding him was the only option. If I used short-distance teleportation, it would take ten times as long to reach our destination.

The city of Lione came into view at last.

The surrounding wall, which had once provided protection from outside forces, had been breached in multiple places. Through these holes, I could see ruined buildings within, still burning. It reminded me a lot of Tagent, back on the southern continent.

I couldn't help but wonder if some of the black husks lying by the breached walls had once been citizens here.

"I've never seen anything like this."

Villiers Fim dropped lower, barely skimming the earth now, and clasped his claws around a man-spider that had noticed us. With one simple motion, he tore it to shreds. The man-spiders might have presented a challenge to humans, but they were no match for a Dragon Lord.

The closer we got to Lione, the more man-spiders and undead soldiers we began seeing, though these were easily dispatched by the Dragon Lord's long, powerful tail.

Once we arrived at the outer wall, Villiers Fim pulled up and slowly circled the city, drawing the attention of the undead inside. Ultimately, our goal was to get them to follow us to where Goemon and Dillan's forces were waiting.

However, if we were to draw out all of the undead at once, I doubted we'd be able to fend them off, not with the haphazard defenses we'd put into place.

To avoid that possibility, we would first lead the undead to a large plain and let loose with a powerful area-of-effect attack to wipe out as many of them as we could. Then it would be up to our forces standing by to take out the remains.

To make sure the undead within the city didn't simply ignore us, we needed to destroy those lurking outside the walls first. That's why we were here.

I felt a little bad for dragging Ariane into this. She looked absolutely miserable. Once she had her feet on the ground again, though, I was certain she'd be back to normal.

I tapped Villiers Fim's leg to give him the signal.

"Let us down here and then continue with the rest of the plan!"

"Leave it to me."

After completing a full circle around the capital, the Dragon Lord dropped close enough to the earth that his tail was practically touching the ground. We shot along at high speed through an empty field on the northeast side of the city. Villiers Fim reached down and dug his front claws into the ground to slow us, ripping two massive channels into the soft dirt.

By some strange happenstance, we managed to stop right next to a pair of undead soldiers. Without a second thought, I unsheathed my Holy Thunder Sword of Caladbolg and struck them down.

"Well, that was a pretty cool landing, if I do say so myself. Whaddya think, Ponta?"

"Kyii?" Ponta popped its head up from my shoulder and shot me a puzzled glance.

In my mind, I fancied myself a bipedal killing machine that had launched into its job as soon as its transport landed. But apparently, Ponta didn't share my romanticism.

I watched Chiyome do a flip through air and land effortlessly on the ground. She made the move look so easy, but I knew it would end in tragedy if I were to try.

Only when Villiers Fim had come to a complete stop did Ariane release her death grip on his leg. As soon as she was on solid ground, she slumped to her knees, shaking slightly. Fortunately, there were no enemies near her, so she could take a moment to collect herself.

But I needed to get to clearing out my own sector.

"Holy Thunder Sword of Caladbolg!"

A surge of purple electricity ran up the masterfully crafted weapon. Blue bolts appeared as well, as a blade of light grew out of it, doubling in size.

The air itself began humming as I swung the glowing sword.

The first enemy to challenge me was one I'd become quite familiar with fighting: a man-spider wielding several club-like weapons. I decided to take it out with a different technique.

"Wyvern Slash!"

Though the enemy was still a fair distance away, due to the added length of my blade, the slash chopped right through the man-spider...and several undead soldiers standing behind it.

The attack had never done anything like that in the game, but now that I knew about it, I figured it could come in handy when facing multiple opponents. It was like a more powerful version of Ponta's grass-cutting wind bursts.

"Kyi kyiiii! Kyi!"

Ponta cheered me on excitedly and wagged its tail, even imitating me by sending out several of its own air bursts. I had to admit, Ponta had gotten quite a bit better at this since we'd started training at the shrine, but it still wouldn't be of much use against the enemies here.

I glanced over at Chiyome to find her taking down one undead soldier after another. Ariane was finally back on her feet too. I watched as she severed the humanoid upper torsos from a man-spider's body and then used her spirt magic to engulf the creature in flames, leaving nothing but charred remains.

Her shoulders were moving up and down in short, controlled breaths, her gaze fixed on her next victim. She seemed to have gotten over the trauma of flying.

Villiers Fim continued making lazy circles around Lione, occasionally diving close to the ground to attack clumps of undead and rip them to shreds, like an eagle pouncing on rabbits.

Unfortunately, we weren't making any noticeable progress, not with the sheer number of troops the undead could bring to bear.

While there were certainly plenty of undead out here beyond the city walls, I knew the numbers within the city limits were far, far greater.

I stole a glance at the top of Lione's defensive wall as I chopped my way through hordes of undead. There was still no sign of anything like the young boy who'd chased after Goemon and his comrades.

From the way Goemon had described the sequence of events, there was no way it had been a normal boy. He had to be someone high up within the church, but other than that, I had no guesses as to who he might have been.

Once we finished clearing out the undead lurking around the city's perimeter, I turned my attention back to the capital. It was oddly quiet.

Ariane stepped up beside me. She seemed to share my concerns.

"That's strange, isn't it? I can still sense the contamination inundating the city, and yet they don't seem to be sending anyone out after us. Think they saw through our plan?"

Chiyome yanked her blade out of an undead soldier and walked over to join us. She tilted her head back and sniffed loudly, raising a suspicious eyebrow.

"The rotting scent is still strong too, so they must still be in there. But still…"

Before I had a chance to ask what she'd picked up on, a powerful gust of wind blew up from behind us, followed by a strong thud that reverberated through the ground. I turned to find Villiers Fim, his wings neatly folded and a concerned expression on his face.

"The forces in the city have formed up and are about to depart."

I looked through one of the massive breaches in Lione's wall. Beyond the mountains of crushed bricks and mortar, I could see dark shadows swarming.

The undead were coming.

Though they weren't as organized as the columns preferred by human armies, they were moving with more cohesion than usual. Something told me that the two figures leading this unholy force were the reason for this.

One of them was a young boy, likely the one Goemon had seen. His hair was trimmed short, just below the ears, and he had a captivating gaze. His face had all the makings of a future heartbreaker, though he still possessed a certain childishness.

His plain white robes were like those worn by members of the priesthood, but given his age, I had a hard time not seeing him as a choirboy.

Even these fine clothes, however, looked like rags compared to those of the man standing next to him.

The man held a scepter carved with intricate patterns—a symbol of his status. Due to the elaborate mitre he wore atop his head, and the thin veil hanging beneath it, it was impossible to see the man's face. Something about his appearance—or lack thereof—filled me with dread.

Hanging from the necks of these two figures were necklaces bearing the symbol of the Hilk religion. It was a pretty safe bet that they were both high-ranking members of the church.

They marched ahead of their endless army of undead and came to a halt as soon as we were all within earshot of each other. The only sound was that of the wind rustling through the grass at our feet.

The veiled man broke the silence. "I didn't expect you to attack with so few people."

His voice was flat and even. I could feel his eyes on me through the veil, and I returned his gaze, to the extent that I could.

"So, you're the silver knight who killed Palurumo, I take it? How interesting... A player who chooses to live on the front lines, foregoing the use of standard tactics. I have to say, it's an honor to finally meet you. Allow me to offer you a little bit of hospitality."

The veiled man raised his hands to the sky and let go of the scepter. I watched it float into the air and spin in a circle as he began chanting.

"Hell King Balam, hear me now! I summon you forth from the underworld!"

A large, black shadow, so dark it seemed to consume all light around it, appeared behind the veiled man. Runes the color of blood snaked across its surface. Moments later, a gargantuan skeleton, around fifteen meters tall, yanked itself out of the shadow. Though I'd never actually seen a demon from hell before, this was pretty much exactly how I would have imagined it.

Two enormous, ram-like horns stuck out of a human skull with four eye sockets, behind which blazed a red flame that seemed to emanate hatred.

Though its body was mostly human in appearance, its torso was covered in matted black hair, while its arms and legs were nothing but bone. From its back extended a pair of charcoal gray wings and a long tail. In one hand, it clutched a large scimitar. It was quite a sight to behold.

The so-called Hell King Balam stretched out its wings with an ominous clack and launched itself at Villiers Fim.

The Dragon Lord responded by darting into the air and catching the blade with his massive claws. He swung his tail like a whip, landing a blow on Balam's torso and throwing it back.

With several powerful thrusts of its wings, the Hell King hovered in midair.

While this battle was being waged above us, the young boy spoke up.

"I am Tismo Ghoula, though you beautiful ladies may call me by my cardinal name, Temprantia."

He shot a charming grin toward Ariane and Chiyome. Then his head began ballooning outward, growing larger and larger until it finally split open, looking like an over-sized anemone. The rest of his body followed suit, his arms stretching into tendrils as several more appendages popped out of his lower torso until he was supported by six thick legs.

Gone was the charming young boy, replaced with a grotesque monster that brought to mind a Venus flytrap.

His six legs hammered into the ground as he barreled forward, whipping a tendril toward Ariane and Chiyome, though they easily dodged it, putting some distance between themselves and this new enemy.

From what I could tell, the boy could move his tendrils at great speed, though he was actually quite slow on his legs. For agile fighters like Ariane and Chiyome, I didn't think this would present much of a problem.

The veiled man raised his scepter again and invoked another spell. "Let me show you what a Magus can do against a Knight! Nether Resonance!"

Another dark shadow appeared, this time beneath the undead army. The eyes of the unmoving soldiers and man-spiders began glowing bright red, and they let out low, bestial cries. As best as I could tell, the spell he'd just cast had powered up his entire army.

Powers similar to this existed in the game, but their area of effect was usually quite limited, and they didn't work on the undead.

The veiled man seemed to be taking pleasure in my reaction. "Coming out here alone was quite reckless."

With a wave of his hand, the legions of undead swarmed forth.

"Wyvern Slash!"

I sent out a blast of energy and chopped through the first man-spider and a dozen or so undead soldiers. This gave me some room, but more kept coming, encircling me.

I unleashed another Wyvern Slash on the soldiers to my right while I used my shield to bash away more on my left, desperately trying to clear a space.

Running low on options, and with waves of undead crashing into me, I used my Holy Thunder Sword of Caladbolg skill and launched a massive Wyvern Slash.

I backed up with each strike to try and put some distance between myself and my opponents, but I knew I couldn't keep going like this forever.

As I battled the undead, I glanced over at the veiled man. For a moment, it felt as if our eyes met.

I could have used teleportation magic to get out of there, but that would have left Ariane and Chiyome alone to face Tismo.

The fastest way out of this would be to cut off the head of the serpent, so to speak.

I jumped back again to put even more distance between myself and the tsunami of undead, using Wyvern Slash after Wyvern Slash to keep them at bay, while trying to draw them away from Ariane and Chiyome.

The veiled man seemed to enjoy watching this battle unfold. But I was about to put an end to all that.

"Dimensional Step!"

I drew the undead army as far away as I could, then used my short-distance teleportation to appear next to the veiled figure.

"Wha?!"

As I'd hoped, this seemed to catch him completely off guard. I smirked to myself as I watched the undead in the distance frantically looking for me. Then I once again used my Holy Thunder Sword of Caladbolg skill to send lightning forking down the blade.

With a powerful swing, I brought the sword down on the veiled man.

CLANG!

A shower of sparks erupted as he swung his scepter up to block my attack, though it still managed to knock him back.

I was impressed. There were few weapons out there that could block the Holy Thunder Sword of Caladbolg. The veiled man seemed even more shaken than I was, though I wasn't about to let my guard down.

"A fighter capable of using magic?! My word! I didn't expect you to be a Paladin."

I tried to land another blow, but he managed to cast a spell before I was able to.

"Evil Thorn!"

Three translucent beings resembling half-rotted corpses appeared out of the tip of his scepter, clacking their jaws ravenously as they advanced on me. I raised my lightning blade to meet them. My sword went right through them, and they vanished in a puff of smoke.

The spell itself didn't pose much of a danger to me, but the veiled man seemed pleased with the results and tried it once more.

This time, I decided to run through the ghastly figures with my shield before launching another strike at the veiled figure.

"Aaugh!"

He shouted in surprise and darted back, barely managing to avoid the tip of my blade. The edge of my sword caught his veil and tore the fabric off.

What was underneath stopped me in my tracks.

An instant later, a black sphere enveloped the once-veiled man and he teleported away. Apparently, he could also use short-distance teleportation magic.

Before I could teleport after him, I noticed several undead closing in on me from all sides. After dispatching them with my sword, and narrowly dodging a blow from a man-spider, I used Dimension Step to get away.

I looked around frantically for the man, but he seemed to have slipped away into the vast hordes of undead.

"There's no way I can spot him from down here."

Everywhere I looked, all I saw were undead. I kept sending Wyvern Slashes into them, but it was about as effective as sprinkling water on a hot stone.

Once I'd managed to clear a bit of space around me, I turned my gaze skyward.

Villiers Fim was still battling the Hell King Balam, but he didn't seem to be having too much difficulty.

Balam would occasionally spit a massive fireball at the Dragon Lord, but Villiers Fim would catch it with a magic-fueled tornado and launch it into the undead soldiers below, incinerating them instantly. Judging by the number of undead bodies littering the battlefield, I got the impression that Villiers Fim was trying to provoke Balam into launching more of these attacks at him.

The Dragon Lord whipped his massive tail out, landing a heavy blow on the Hell King's arm and sending his scimitar flying down into the crowd, chopping a man-spider clean in two. The blade evaporated in a puff of oily gray smoke.

Balam looked down, exposing himself to another wind attack from Villiers Fim. The tornado chopped Balam's tail and one of his wings clean off.

"Hmph, I hardly even worked up a sweat."

The Dragon Lord grabbed Balam's head and threw him to the ground with tremendous force. The Hell King crashed into the undead soldiers below, sending bodies flying every which way.

Balam tried flapping his remaining wing a few times, but he couldn't make it back into the air. If he were to continue facing Villiers Fim like this, he'd be done for.

I checked in on Ariane and Chiyome and, fortunately, it looked like they had their own battle pretty well wrapped up.

To make up for his slow speed, Cardinal Tismo had focused on using the tendrils sprouting from his body to try and smash the two women while simultaneously blasting acid from the tendrils growing out of his head.

Unfortunately for him, Ariane and Chiyome were too good at reading his movements and easily dodged all of his attacks. In between, they darted in to land blows of their own.

By the time I started watching, he'd already lost one of the large tendrils that had once been his arm and was using the other to try and chase down Ariane. Chiyome came in from behind and, using her spirit magic, launched a water spear right through his stomach, temporarily stopping his pursuit.

Ariane wasn't about to let an opportunity like that go to waste. After deftly dodging the tendril, she chopped it clean off as it swung past her.

Tismo's body began to shudder, and an ominous moan rose from the anemone-like object growing out of his head.

Ariane and Chiyome stood at the ready, waiting for him to make his next move. Before their very eyes, new tendrils began growing out of the stumps. In a matter of seconds, it was like he'd never lost them at all, though the injury to his stomach remained. My guess was that he could only regenerate the tendrils.

Ariane and Chiyome picked up on this too, and immediately changed their tactics.

Ariane moved to flank him, while Chiyome faced him head-on, attracting all of his attention.

As Ariane got close, Tismo spewed acid out of his head to keep her away. She dodged these attacks and scored another few hits onto his body.

Meanwhile, the cardinal continued pursuing Chiyome, following her every movement, just as she'd hoped. She jumped to the side, causing the tendrils to cross over one another. Summoning a water spear, she stabbed straight through where the tendrils overlapped, pinning them to the earth. To make sure they were good and stuck, she repeated the process two more times.

Ariane closed in again, this time with her sword engulfed in flames, and thrust the blade deep into Tismo's stomach. He let loose a horrible, inhuman scream.

It was unlikely that a simple blow like that would prove fatal to such a large creature, but it was clear that, one way or another, Tismo wasn't leaving this battle alive. Ariane and Chiyome were just too good.

I turned my attention back to the undead hordes and discovered a man-spider lunging at me. Using Dimensional Step a few times, I managed to put a fair bit of distance between myself and the soldiers.

I took up a position away from Villiers Fim, Ariane, and Chiyome to try and find the veiled man again, keeping an eye out for any undead that happened to get close.

I thought back on the first thing the veiled man had said to me: *"So, you're the silver knight who killed Palurumo, I take it?"*

The logical conclusion was that Palurumo worked for him. And since Palurumo served directly below the ruler of the Holy Hilk Kingdom, that could only mean that the veiled man was the pontiff himself.

I never would have expected to run across him here on the battlefield, but the more I thought about it, the more it made sense. He was the one, after all, who'd used his dark magic to create the undead in the first place.

Something else the pontiff said had also caught my interest. I hadn't had much time to dwell on it, since we were in the middle of combat, but now that I had a moment to myself, I was able to think about it more.

If my hunch was correct, then that meant defeating the pontiff might be out of the question.

After cutting away his veil, I'd caught a quick glimpse of the pontiff's face...or rather, where his face should have been. In its place was a skull, with a deep red flame burning behind the empty eye sockets. Almost the same as what was under my own helmet.

We were a lot more similar than I cared to admit.

The next time we met, I wanted to ask him one simple question: Why was he doing this?

I looked around at all the undead and figured it was finally time I did something about them.

"I figured it'd come down to this, even if I'd been hoping to avoid it."

I picked Ponta up off my neck.

"Listen, buddy, can you stay out of the way for a bit? This next attack's gonna be kinda powerful, and I'm worried about you."

"Kyiiiii!" Ponta took off into the sky, looking like dandelion fluff adrift on the wind.

I took a deep breath and prepared to execute my next spell.

"Open the doors of heaven and send Archangel Savior Uriel down to me!"

A moment later, I felt as if nearly all of my magic power had been sucked out of my body as twin halos of light appeared at my feet. Stone pillars began shooting out of the ground to form a wall of sorts.

The undead closest to me were torn to shreds, one after another, as circles of light appeared at their feet, purifying them and turning their bodies into sparks that shot into the sky.

A golden pillar so bright that I had to avert my eyes jutted up from the ground, and I could hear voices singing hymns in perfect harmony. An immense figure stepped off the pillar, standing around five meters tall—the same height as the Executioner, Archangel Michael.

In contrast with the absolutely flawless golden armor worn by Michael the Executioner, Uriel the Savior was covered in heavily battered golden armor, like something a battle-seasoned knight would wear. This matched the unadorned helmet on his head and the mammoth war hammer at his back, the latter of which was somehow longer than he was tall.

Six glorious wings made of beautiful, shining feathers graced his back.

This was one of my four Paladin skills, Archangel Savior Uriel.

The angel of legend tilted his head back and looked up at the sky before letting out an ear-splitting howl. The soundwave kicked up all the undead on the plain like dust in a wind storm. They, too, turned to light and disappeared in bright flashes.

It was truly a sight to behold.

The stone wall that had surrounded us had faded, and once again I was granted an unobstructed view of the battlefield.

Uriel shrank to around two meters and clung tightly to my back.

"Aaaaaaaaaauuuuuuuuuuuugggh!!!"

Out of the corner of my eye, I caught sight of Ponta looping around in the air overhead, looking down at me with great concern.

Just like last time, I couldn't help but scream as the immense force enveloped my body. No matter how many times I experienced this, there was no way I could get used to it. All I could do was grit my teeth and try to hang on to my sanity.

I squeezed my hand into a fist and pressed down hard on my thigh as I pushed myself back to my feet.

My breath came heavy under the pressure of the mythical creature. I watched in silence as the surviving undead continued their relentless advance.

The entire undead army was descending on me this time around, so I wouldn't need to worry about executing any large-scale attacks like I had back in Saureah.

If I played my cards right, I could take them all out in one go, then disable the Paladin skill.

I took several deep breaths to focus, then I felt Uriel's massive wings flap behind me, lifting me high into the air.

Villiers Fim, realizing what was about to happen, discarded Balam's corpse and swooped down to grab Ariane and Chiyome before flying high into the air.

"Kyii!" Ponta also seemed to understand that something big was up, and it swooped down to land atop my helmet.

The Paladin skills were such that they would pretty much annihilate anything within a given area. I did my best to place myself somewhere that would provide the maximum impact with as little collateral damage as possible, but I'd never actually used this skill before so I couldn't be sure.

I called out the attack. "Meteor Ray Destruction!"

Uriel screamed to the heavens and hefted his massive hammer. Massive blasts of light shot out from the clouds, tracing lines across the sky before slamming into the ground with such incredible force that it sent the undead soldiers flying.

Over and over, each ray hit the ground and exploded into a bright flash of light.

Just when I thought the aerial bombardment was over, another, larger object appeared in the sky. It was an enormous mass of burning rock, so large that it almost looked like a small hill ripped from the countryside. At the moment of collision, my vision went white.

The next thing I knew, a powerful shockwave rolled past me, followed by scorching heat and a rush of sand and stones.

I coughed hard, struggling to breathe.

"Well, that was far more powerful than the Archangel Michael. They really should banish that kind of magic."

I waved the dust away from my face as Uriel clung to my back. I had to squint to see anything.

"Kyiii! Kiiiiii!"

Ponta did its part by using its feather-duster-like tail to keep the dust away from my helmet, though this also blew dust up its nose, sending the poor thing into a sneezing fit, which it immediately followed with a bout of self-grooming.

Merifully, a breeze swept in and carried away much of the dust, and I finally got a clear look at the damage.

Where an army of undead had once stood was now a massive crater of scorched earth.

"The meteor did that much damage?"

I could hardly believe my eyes at the show of immense power, or rather, wanton destruction before me. Looking out over the ravaged plains, I could only spot a few clusters of undead. In fact, it looked like the only survivors were the man-spiders; none of the undead infantry were still standing. If this was all that was left, I didn't see a need for calling in the reinforcements.

However, I couldn't help but notice that the veiled man was suspiciously absent. I was confident that he hadn't died in the blast, especially considering that he could teleport. Between when I summoned the attack and the impact itself, he would have had more than enough time to get away.

Something told me that the next time the pontiff and I met, it would be in Fehrbio Alsus, the capital of the Holy Hilk Kingdom.

I turned my gaze west, but the Rutios Mountains formed an impenetrable wall, blocking my view of the holy lands.

CHAPTER 3
Amassing Forces

𝒯HE CENTRAL CATHEDRAL in Alsus—home to Pontiff Thanatos Sylvius Hilk, the leader of the Holy Hilk Kingdom—was situated deep in the Rutios mountain range. It was a magnificent building covered in a gleaming white façade and surrounded by an open-air corridor.

The white stone floor was polished to such a magnificent sheen that it could serve as a mirror, reflecting perfectly the ceiling above and the beautiful religious scenes painted across it. Grand chandeliers hung from the ceiling at regular intervals.

All these gorgeous works of art spoke to the Holy Hilk Kingdom's long history, expansion, and rise to power.

But there was more inside.

In the confines of the cathedral sat an empty room that no follower of the Hilk had ever set foot inside.

In the blink of an eye, a man dressed in elaborate, priestly robes appeared within.

The sign of the Hilk hung from the man's neck, and he held an intricately decorated scepter in one hand. This was the master of this cathedral and the ruler of the entire Hilk Kingdom, Pontiff Thanatos.

He let out a ragged sigh.

However, his face showed no emotion. The man, after all, had neither face nor flesh attached to his barren skull, only the mitre that identified his status within the church.

From the mitre dangled the remains of a veil, under which gaped two vacant eye sockets, behind which a red flame, the manifestation of his soul, flickered ominously.

"What the hell was that?!"

Though by all appearances he looked undead, there was something decidedly human about the way he spoke. His yells echoed throughout the empty cathedral.

Earlier that day, Thanatos had traveled to one of his recently conquered cities, the capital of Lione in the Delfrent Kingdom. He'd gone there to bolster the ranks of his undead armies.

Imbuing human corpses with a rune stone and summoning the same dark spell over and over again was simple, if tedious, work.

It felt like a waste of his time and talent to have to create each and every piece of cannon fodder one by one. However, when he stepped back and looked at the huge forces he'd amassed, it all seemed worth it. It might have been menial work, but it was fulfilling.

There was also, of course, the other recent development, which had helped break up the pontiff's monotonous life and given him something to focus his attention on.

It felt like several lifetimes ago that he'd somehow transferred from the virtual world and found himself stranded here. It was tough going at first, but he was unmatched in this world. Through diligent effort, he'd managed to carve out a place of power for himself.

Not too long ago, he'd lost the first of his most powerful disciples, one of the seven cardinals, in a land that he'd already conquered.

Thanatos had grown convinced that the only person who could have killed the cardinal was someone like himself—another player from the game. He was elated at the thought of meeting another outsider.

However, as this player continued killing his cardinals one by one, the pontiff decided it was time to offer them a warm welcome.

Having lived in this world for so long without interacting with anyone else from the old world, something inside Thanatos longed to battle his opponent to the death. This was probably due to his competitiveness as a gamer. Win or lose, it would be an exciting match.

Just the thought of such an encounter made even tedious task of building an army enjoyable. It was like he was playing the game all over again.

Things had really begun to kick off when a dragon showed up that morning. Thanatos had been busy transforming dead humans into soldiers, in his newly conquered domain of Lione.

He couldn't remember the last time he'd seen a dragon, but recalled that there were some players who could control and even ride them. However, the cost of owning and maintaining a dragon was far higher than that of undead soldiers. Sure, they looked impressive, but the cost versus payout was pretty poor.

When he caught sight of the humanoid figures clutching the dragon's hind legs, that's when he knew this was no mere monster roaming the skies.

After doing several loops around Lione, possibly to gauge Thanatos's strength, the dragon had landed to the west of the city.

Thanatos had smirked under his veil. The other player who had come all the way to the Delfrent Kingdom didn't even realize that he was here.

He called the majority of his forces back into the city and left a small contingent outside the walls to keep the enemy busy.

A dragon alone was hardly enough to level the playing field against the pontiff's undead soldiers and specter warriors. Moreover, he had one of his cardinals, Tismo, with him. The dragon would be dead in a matter of moments.

Generally, you only enter into battle against a dragon with the understanding that you're going to lose a great deal of your troops, but the pontiff had more than a few tricks up his sleeve. There was no way he'd lose this fight.

For starters, he could summon one of his demons to weaken the dragon enough to allow the specter warriors to overpower it. All he had to do was knock the dragon down a peg or two, and then the battle would get interesting.

His plan formed, Thanatos drew his army of undead back through the shattered walls that had once protected Lione.

With a powerful dragon backing them up, the small group of fighters must have thought they were a sufficient force for reconnaissance. If anything, it spoke to their bravery.

Once within the city's wall, Thanatos was surprised when he looked out again and found the bodies of his undead soldiers and specter warriors littering the ground. He could count only a few left standing despite the relatively large force he'd left to defend the perimeter.

Even more surprising, though, were the three people standing with the dragon. One of them was a large knight clad from head to toe in silver armor, while the other two were an elf and a beast girl—species that the Holy Hilk Kingdom had spent years trying to eradicate.

Could this be the silver knight he'd heard reports about? The one who'd killed his cardinal? By some strange twist of fate, here they both were.

The knight's armor was accented with intricate white and blue designs. On his back fluttered a black cape, and he wielded a magnificent sword and beautifully decorated shield. He looked like a hero straight out of a legend.

At first glance, Thanatos knew this man was no mere soldier. Underneath his veil, his skeletal jaw contorted in an imitation of a smile.

He'd never expected to just happen across the other player like this, and especially not so soon. The knight looked over in his direction, and the pontiff's heart began racing.

It didn't seem like the knight was about to charge into battle, so Thanatos considered talking to him face to face.

It was time for him to greet his new friends...and do something about that dragon.

However, since the other player was evidently a Knight, while Thanatos himself was a Magus, he wouldn't stand a chance if this battle turned physical. But being so close to his domain also gave Thanatos something of an advantage. He decided it was best to strike the opening blow.

Things went off exactly as planned. The pontiff's Hell King Balam took on the dragon while Tismo went about killing the two women.

This left the human player to face off against the pontiff and his legions.

To stack the deck even further in his favor, Thanatos called upon Nether Resonance to make his soldiers go berserk. While this reduced his ability to control them, it greatly increased their attack power. With an army this large, the other player wouldn't stand a chance, no matter powerful he was.

It would be unfortunate to kill the other player before they even had the chance to speak, but Thanatos figured the knight would retreat before that could happen. After all, he was up against an overwhelming army, and he shouldn't have any particular attachment to this land.

But if the knight stayed, and Thanatos took him down, then at least the other player would be sent to the battle results screen and could figure out what had happened to him. Once there, he should be able to contact the developers, and things would ultimately play out the same for Thanatos.

The pontiff raised his hand, sending forth wave after wave of undead. As he watched, the knight retreated, and he felt all the more assured of his victory.

That changed almost immediately, however, when the silver knight suddenly reappeared at the pontiff's side, swinging his heavy blade. Thanatos just barely managed to block the blow with his scepter, though the force of it still threw him back. A Magus could hardly stand up against a prolonged physical assault.

Back when Thanatos had started the game, he'd been presented with two options: to be a magical- or physical-attack character. Yet the player standing in front of him seemed to be a combination of both.

He felt annoyance wash over him at the thought that a new feature had been added without his knowledge.

Thanatos tried using Evil Thorn to hold off his opponent and suss out his weaknesses, but the results were surprising. The attack seemed to be especially ineffective against the silver knight.

He followed with another Evil Thorn, though the knight came striking back hard. His sword was now far bigger than it had been before, and he was swinging straight for Thanatos's neck.

Only a hair's breadth separated the pontiff from certain death. He barely made it.

At the time, Thanatos hadn't understood why the silver knight paused his attack, but he decided not to dwell on it and quickly teleported into the middle of one of his armies. The undead dutifully shuffled around him, shielding him from sight.

He may have gotten away for now, but he still wasn't safe. Thanatos kept teleporting, bouncing around to various locations until he was back in Lione.

Usually when a small force went up against a much more powerful army, the best strategy was to kill their leadership, and it looked like that was exactly what the silver knight was trying to do: teleport in close and try to cut the commander down with a single blow. It was an effective strategy for a Mystic Knight to use against a Magus.

In that case, the pontiff's best defense was to simply stay out of his opponent's line of sight, as short-distance teleportation required that you be able to see where you wanted to go. With all the undead soldiers filling the battlefield, teleportation should prove difficult, if not impossible.

Then, Thanatos would just have to sit back and wait for his berserking soldiers to tear the man apart.

At least, that was what he had hoped would happen.

But within a matter of minutes, Thanatos watched as the tide of the battle turned in an utterly unexpected direction.

Hell King Balam, a demon he'd put a lot of energy into summoning, had fought a tough battle against the massive dragon, though it was growing clear that Balam was on the losing end.

Tismo Ghoula Temprantia wasn't faring much better against the two despicable non-humans. They fought too well together for him to put up any kind of meaningful resistance.

The pontiff returned his gaze to the silver knight and was taken aback by what he saw.

Though the knight had originally retreated in the face of so many berserking undead, after teleporting away, he'd executed a powerful magic attack.

The Magus class differed from physical classes in that it specialized in magical attacks with a wide area of effect. Yet here was this Mystic Knight, summoning an angel the likes of which Thanatos had never seen.

And that was just the beginning.

The knight called forth a meteor shower, killing at least half of the undead. He followed this up with a more focused meteor strike, scarring the very earth. With these two attacks, the pontiff's army had been completely annihilated.

"Wh-what was that?" Thanatos's question hung in the air, unanswered.

What he'd witnessed went beyond a mere overpowered player character. Being able to wipe out an entire army on your own didn't just harm the *balance* of the game, it decimated the game's very mechanics.

If players could become this powerful, then there was no sense bothering with subordinate team members—or even armies—in the first place.

Even more troubling, the player's comrades possessed impressive abilities in their own right, making simple work of the pontiff's minions. There was something wrong with this whole scenario.

One thing was certain...if the system administrators knew about this, then they were utterly incompetent.

On the other hand, if they were unaware, then that meant the silver knight had hacked his character. Anger welled within the pontiff at the thought. His grip tightened around his scepter, and he rapped it on the stone floor.

Still, forcing an entirely new hacked class like the Mystic Knight into the game would have been no simple task. More likely, the class itself had been designed by the developers and the player had illegally altered his character's stats.

Still atop Lione's defensive wall, Thanatos reached into his robe and pulled out a transportation stone. The tiny gem, just small enough to fit comfortably in the palm of his hand, gave off a haunting purple glow.

Transportation stones allowed their users to take advantage of special teleportation platforms to move between locations. The only catch was that these locations were fixed. But they allowed for greater flexibility than short-distance teleportation magic, which required line of sight.

This came at a cost, of course, as each use consumed one of these rare gems.

Without a second thought, Thanatos threw the precious gem to the ground. A magic rune appeared at his feet as it shattered, and a moment later, he was back in the Alsus cathedral.

Thanatos immediately made his way toward the vault in his private chambers. Inside, he reached for another transportation stone and paused. His supply was running short.

"I'll need to make some more."

He took one of the stones and threw it at his feet. An instant later, the gleaming cathedral was replaced with a dimly lit office.

Shelves lined the walls, stuffed with books all the way up to the ceiling. Even more volumes were stacked haphazardly across the office floor, leaning towers of knowledge ready to topple at any moment. At the far end of the room was a large, wooden desk.

A young, muscular man with dark bags under his eyes sat behind the desk. Despite being in his twenties, his unkempt blond hair and unshaven face gave him the appearance of an old man.

As soon as the man saw Thanatos, he rushed over.

"Is something the matter, Your Holiness?"

This man was Cardinal Marcos Invidia Humanitas, who spent much of his time in Alsus here in his study.

Marcos's surprise was understandable. It was incredibly rare for the pontiff to use a transportation stone to visit the cardinal's study.

Even more baffling was the fact that the pontiff's veil had been torn away, revealing his lack of face underneath. The cardinal hurried to a drawer and retrieved the extra veil he kept on hand.

Thanatos attached it to his mitre. "I want you to release Aamon and Mammon from the basement, then dispatch all of our remaining undead soldiers and specter warriors to close off the city."

Cardinal Marcos gulped audibly at this. Aamon and

Mammon were two spirit creatures that the pontiff had created as a last resort weapon against his enemies. Even the more powerful cardinals paled in comparison to them.

They'd been sealed off to keep them from wreaking havoc. Once that seal was lifted, there'd be no going back.

The pontiff's authorization to unleash them could only mean that the Holy Hilk Kingdom was in grave danger.

The last Marcos had heard, the Holy Hilk Kingdom's simultaneous invasions of its neighbors had been going well. He'd felt annoyed at being left behind to keep watch over the capital while his comrades served on the front lines, but such was his lot.

Sensing his underling's confusion, the pontiff explained. "I can no longer feel Augrent. Did the invasion to the south also fail? But I can still feel Elin. What's going on?"

Marcus was shocked to hear that his fellow cardinals had fallen.

Thanatos searched deep within himself, tugging at the spiritual threads that connected him to his cardinals, but it was still the same. He could no longer feel Cardinal Augrent, nor could he pinpoint Cardinal Elin's location. It was utterly baffling.

What exactly had happened in the Salma Kingdom?

Considering how easily the silver knight's comrades had held their own against Tismo, it wasn't out of the realm of believability that similar creatures had taken down his other cardinals. Thanatos gritted his teeth as these dark thoughts flooded his mind.

The silver knight would almost certainly be making his way here shortly. As it stood, the pontiff's likelihood of survival seemed fairly low. But he wasn't ready to give up, not after so many years living in this game. No, he'd bring all the power he could muster and strike back.

"I'd like to assemble the remaining cardinals here to bolster our forces, but there's no guarantee that he won't strike while we gather them. If they send a small force by dragon, they could be here tomorrow, or possibly even today. Marcos, do you think you can handle it?"

Thanatos lifted his veil slightly, the glowing flame within his empty skull reflecting in the cardinal's eyes. Marcos nodded solemnly.

The holy city he'd vowed to protect was now under attack. His heart swelled at the opportunity to prove himself in battle—to not only the pontiff, but to all those who'd doubted him. He would save the Holy Hilk Kingdom in its darkest hour.

Marcos bowed his head low and silently thanked the gods for granting him this chance.

If they were going to unleash the sealed beasts, then something would need to be done about Alsus's citizens. But first, Cardinal Marcos needed to assemble the specter warriors. He strode from the room.

After watching the other man leave, Thanatos made his way over to the open window and looked down at the holy capital.

It was a clean, well-organized city, filled with thousands of smiling people going about their day.

He felt a twinge of regret, knowing the city he'd built would fall to ruin at the hands of Aamon and Mammon, but this was what they'd been created for. Thanatos had known this day would come eventually.

"Even if the game is over, this city can at least put up a good fight. It will serve its purpose. Whoever you are, silver knight, I hope you're ready to take on my entire kingdom."

A hollow laugh echoed out from behind Thanatos's thin veil. Then he turned his back on the city and headed deep into the bowels of the cathedral to remove the seal on Aamon and Mammon.

Here in Lione, the once-lively city lay shrouded in oppressive silence. Even after the relentless undead assault, much of the capital remained standing, despite the invaders' best efforts to level it.

Squares lined with shops the residents had patronized were now filled with their bodies. It was an awful sight to behold.

The only signs of life, if you could even call them that, were the few surviving undead soldiers and man-spiders roaming the streets, but we dispatched them with relative ease.

Even though I wasn't able to sense the undead like Ariane and Chiyome, Ponta would wag its tail as soon as it caught the scent of one of these creatures. Following its nose, it would eventually lead me to an enemy, so at least I wouldn't be caught totally off-guard.

"Kyii!"

Ponta had found an undead soldier half buried in the remains of a building, which I quickly dispatched with a single thrust from my sword. After making sure the coast was clear, I glanced around to get my bearings.

Much to my surprise, I found Ariane standing nearby, staring straight at me. "Are you even listening, Arc?"

She had her hands on her hips and her back arched, emphasizing her ample bosom. My gaze naturally fell to her gently bouncing chest.

Even though I was wearing a helmet, she somehow

knew where I was looking. I could practically see the anger welling up within her, so I scratched the back of my head in embarrassment and returned my eyes to hers.

"Oh, uh...hey, Ariane! What brings you here?"

She glared at me. Apparently, I wasn't as good at playing it cool as I'd thought.

"I'll repeat myself, but just this once. I was asking you to show a little consideration and *tell* someone before you use an attack like that! You almost killed me and Chiyome!"

I bowed my head in apology. She had every right to be angry.

I had absolutely no idea just how massive Uriel's attacks would be, though I probably could have guessed. Evidently, "savior" wasn't just some fancy title.

The problem was that Paladin abilities were all so massively powerful. They put such an enormous strain on my mind and body that I couldn't just try them out on a whim.

Archangel Guardian Raphael and Archangel Prophet Gabriel were still untested, but there was a chance I'd need to use them in the upcoming battle with the Hilk.

I cocked my head to the side in thought, but quickly thought better of it as I felt Ponta begin sliding off my helmet.

Ariane gave an exasperated sigh as she watched me mull things over. I could tell she was equal parts exhausted and annoyed. Fortunately, Chiyome chose that moment to arrive and save me.

She noiselessly hopped down from the roof she'd been standing on to survey the city. Her tail twitched behind her.

"You shouldn't be too strict with him, Ariane. If it weren't for Arc, we'd still be fighting the other undead. He got us out of that battle with no injuries."

I stepped closer to Chiyome, my sole defender. However, Ariane wasn't finished. She narrowed her eyes and pointed an accusatory finger in my direction.

"No, no, no! You can't just let him off the hook like that, Chiyome! If you don't drill it into Arc's thick skull, then he'll never understand. He tore up the earth right in front of us! Who knows what could've happened if he'd missed!"

I looked to Chiyome for more support, but she only shook her head.

"I suppose she's right there."

All I could do was bow my head and ask for forgiveness. "I promise to be more careful in the future."

Ariane shrugged her shoulders and let out a loud, exaggerated sigh before turning her gaze upward. It looked like something else was troubling her.

"You know, ever since you two fought, Villiers Fim alternates between speaking to you as if you're best friends and as if you were somehow higher status than him. Isn't that odd?"

I followed her gaze to find the Dragon Lord flying in slow circles above the capital. I thought back on our relationship and couldn't help but agree.

I must have gained his respect by showing myself equal to, or even more powerful than him. The real question was how our relationship would develop going forward. After all, I had little experience in these matters.

After the battle had ended, Villiers Fim had told me he'd keep watch above the city, and launched into the sky without another word.

"Kyii?" Ponta's mewing interrupted my thoughts. It had picked up on something.

I looked around to see what had drawn Ponta's attention. My gaze settled on a member of the Jinshin clan standing alone on a rooftop nearby. Like Chiyome, she jumped down soundlessly and hurried over to me.

"Goemon says he's found what he believes to be survivors, but they're trapped behind some rubble. Could you please come back with me and assist us?"

The young woman was dressed in the same black garb as Chiyome and wore a nervous look on her face.

"Of course. Please, lead the way."

The young Jinshin warrior nodded once and started off. Like Villiers Fim, she was also being overly polite.

"People really are laying it on thick huh?"

I hadn't been saying this to anyone in particular, but Ariane's ears perked up, and she elbowed me lightly in the side as we walked.

"Isn't that what I said? They're acting like you're one of the Dragon Lords now. It makes sense, I guess, considering how you wiped out all those undead on your own. Plus, we didn't even get to use the defensive line we spent so much time making."

We'd built it under the assumption that we'd be facing a battle brimming with disorganized enemies, like we had back in Saureah. However, when the opportunity to draw all of the undead together and wipe them out with a single blow presented itself, I knew I had to take it. It was a better outcome overall, but it still felt bittersweet.

We'd carefully selected our fighting positions and had gone through so much effort to earn the support of the elves and Jinshin clan, and yet we hadn't even used them. I could only imagine how demoralizing that was.

To a relative novice in military affairs like myself, though, a great victory meant ending the battle quickly, without needing to call reinforcements or suffer any casualties.

Up ahead, I saw the young cat person step into a garden and rush over to a building that looked as if it had collapsed during a fire.

The building had a rather austere appearance, as if someone had made a half-hearted attempt to turn a storehouse into a home. What had once been the second floor and roof had completely collapsed into a pile of bricks.

I spotted Goemon and several other muscular mountain people from the Jinshin clan, dressed in their familiar ninja garb, standing in front of the house. The group nodded to me as I approached. I felt like a foreman entering a construction site, ready to give orders.

Goemon stepped forward and, as had become our custom, raised his hand to bump my fist before jerking his chin toward the rubble.

"There."

He wasn't a man of many words, but he got the message across.

Many of the bricks had been hauled away from the area he indicated, and there was a large boulder blocking the entrance to what appeared to be a basement.

Chiyome walked over, her ears twitching. "I can sense some of our people down there."

I gave her a quizzical look. "Due to the heavy influence of the Hilk teachings here, I would've figured that all of the mountain people were run out of town. Then again, there were quite a few living in secret back in Nohzan too."

I thought of all the mountain people we'd set free back in Saureah. Even under the watchful eye of the Holy Hilk Kingdom, the most widely followed religion among humans, there would always be those who defied the church's teachings.

Examining the large boulder blocking the basement, I couldn't help but think that Goemon could've moved it himself. But it was big enough that he might've had to muscle it out of the way, risking debris falling on those below.

If Goemon, his warriors, and I all joined in together, we could probably lift it straight up, a much safer option.

Just as I was about to get into position, I saw a middle-aged man's face appear in a gap between the boulder and the opening.

"Help's finally arrived! Hurry up so I can get outta here! I've been trapped for so long I thought I was done for!"

The eager man's face was dingy, covered in dirt and sweat. However, he looked distinctly human to me, and not one of the mountain people, as Chiyome had claimed.

I turned back to Ariane, Chiyome, and Goemon, hoping to get some feedback on the best course of action.

But I was met with frowns from the two women and crossed arms from Goemon.

Personally, I thought this kind of job was best suited to Villiers Fim. However, he was currently enjoying keeping watch up in the air, and it didn't seem like he planned on coming down anytime soon.

"Well, it's not doing us any good to just stand around doing nothing. Let's get this boulder out of the way."

Goemon and three of his warriors stepped forward.

"All right, on three..."

After everyone had a grip, I gave the count, and we lifted in unison. The boulder was a lot lighter than I'd expected. When we dropped it in its new resting place nearby, the ground shook with the impact. Apparently, it *wasn't* all that light—the Jinshin warriors were just that strong.

"Aw'right, finally! Dunno what took you guys so long. I've been stuck down there for days, I'll have y'know!"

With the entrance now unblocked, the man came crawling out of the basement. He brushed the dust off his clothes as he stood, a look of annoyance on his face. His gaze froze on Goemon.

"Wait, what's going on here? Beastmen...and elves?! Who are you guys?"

The man was probably forty years old or so and, despite the filth covering his body, he was dressed rather elaborately. Between that and his entitled demeanor, I reasoned he was a member of the nobility.

The man let out a blood curdling scream when he saw the burnt-out remains of his house.

"Nooooooo! What happened to my home?! Why, God, why?!"

We all watched as the man slumped to his knees and continued screaming unintelligibly. He clearly hadn't grasped the enormity of the assault his city had suffered.

Ariane glowered at the man. "God, you're a fool."

She turned her attention to me.

"Let's leave this pathetic excuse for a man here and check out what's down below. I've got a bad feeling about this."

Without another word, she hurried down the stairs with Chiyome on her heels. Ponta mewed agitatedly for me to join them.

"Kyii! Kyiiiii!"

I shot a quick glance back at Goemon, but he only offered a simple nod in response. He'd stand watch over the noble and leave the investigation up to us. I took off after Ariane.

At the bottom of the short stairwell, we found ourselves in a spacious room with a large bed in the center. The room had a musty odor to it.

On top of the bed lay a cat woman, her wrists bound by metal clasps affixed to the wall. It was a scene very similar to one I'd witnessed back in the Rhoden Kingdom.

Ariane suddenly seemed very aware of my presence and hurriedly yanked the sheets off the bed to cover the naked woman.

"Could you, like, look away or something, Arc?"

I quickly averted my gaze and looked around the room instead.

In one of the corners stood a shelf built into the wall, on which sat a crystal lamp, some alcohol, and what I could only assume were snacks.

Next to the shelves was a small cooking area, where I spotted smoked meat, a knife, and some other utensils.

With all of the supplies down here, I figured the man could've survived a while longer with little trouble. The only question was whether the woman was actually being given any of this food.

By the way she was chained to the bed, it seemed likely she was a slave. Would an entitled member of the nobility share his limited food with someone he saw as property?

The question didn't even need to be asked.

"I can't find the key to the handcuffs..."

Chiyome had torn apart the area surrounding the bed and was still coming up short, so I walked over to the wall where the chains were fastened and broke them free. The sound of rending metal echoed throughout the room.

As I stepped forward to cast a curative spell on the woman and heal the bruises covering her body, I saw Chiyome's cat ears twitch. Her eyes darted around the room.

"There's a hidden chamber in here somewhere."

"Kyii!" Ponta seemed to concur.

I set my furry companion down and followed Chiyome over to the shelf built into the wall and gave it a hard push. Much to my surprise, it slid backward on the stone flooring, revealing a hidden room.

Ariane gasped. "Wow, Chiyome, how did you know?"

Chiyome's ears flittered. "It wasn't anything special. The echo of the breaking chains didn't sound right."

She turned her gaze back to the dimly lit room, grabbed the crystal lamp, and stepped inside. Before I could follow her in, Ariane put up a hand to stop me.

"We'll check this room out. Arc, could you help the woman?"

I turned and made my way back to the woman on the bed.

I tore the handcuffs away from her wrists, then cast Heal and gave her a quick once-over. She seemed to be breathing all right, though she didn't do more than stare at the ceiling above. I hoped she was only tired.

It was then that I noticed a rather powerful stench coming from the room Chiyome and Ariane had disappeared into. I felt a weight forming in the pit of my stomach as my mind cycled through possible sources for the rotting smell.

Movement on the bed caught my eye. I turned back, but the woman was nowhere to be seen. I looked around to try and find her, but Chiyome had taken the only light source, making it nearly impossible for me to see more than a few feet.

"Ariane, I can't find her!"

Ariane stepped out of the hidden room and began frantically looking for the woman.

"What?! She was just here a moment ago, wasn't she?"

The room wasn't all that large, so I figured that she must have rolled off the side of the bed and was now crouching there. As I leaned over to check, I heard a scream coming from outside.

"Gyaaaaaaaaaaaaaaaaugh!"

Ariane and I jerked our heads toward the stairs in unison.

"Outside, now!"

She bolted out of the room. As I tried to follow, my leg caught the side of the bed, sending splinters everywhere.

Back in the light of day, we found the cat woman dressed in a negligee and holding a knife in her hand. She was covered in blood, and her shoulders were shaking.

The noble lay on the ground, his throat slashed.

The woman dropped the knife and slumped down to her knees. "This... This bastard, he... My sister! My little sister! Right in front of me!"

No one knew what to say.

A moment later, Chiyome appeared at the top of the stairs behind us. She spoke matter-of-factly as she dimmed the crystal lamp.

"She was the only survivor."

That was all we needed to hear.

The man had been keeping this woman and others locked away down there.

It was clear to me now that my idealistic notion of simply setting the mountain people free, like King Asparuh had done back in the Nohzan Kingdom, wouldn't simply fix decades of slavery. It was going to take a lot of work.

This made me wonder what kind of impact destroying the Holy Hilk Kingdom would have.

I recalled the skeletal face of the pontiff—a face much like my own—and shook my head. That, too, wouldn't just solve all our problems.

There would only be minor changes with the fall of the Hilk. Just as it had taken time for the rift to form between all these species, so too would it take time to repair it. A depressing prospect.

Ariane walked to the woman's side and gently urged her away from the body of her blood-soaked captor.

I looked up at the massive capital around us and was suddenly struck by how massive the place was. There had to be a fair number of survivors hidden within the wreckage, but I didn't have time to spare on them just now.

I figured I could leave Ariane, Chiyome, and Goemon behind to oversee rescue operations.

Dillan and I would return to the Nohzan Kingdom, report on the results of our battle, and then make our way to the Salma Kingdom to check on progress there.

As for Villiers Fim...well, I figured we could leave him here for now.

There was a lot to do.

Princess Riel was the first person to greet us as Dillan and I teleported into the Nohzan Kingdom. She came rushing over with her two bodyguards once she received word that we were back in the castle, and her eyes went wide with joy when she heard our report on the events back in Delfrent.

"Wow, I can't believe it's all over so quickly! I knew we could count on you, Arc!"

It felt good to be praised by the young princess.

With that out of the way, I left Dillan in Saureah and used Transport Gate to make my way to the fort on the border between the Salma Kingdom and Brahniey, where our forces had prepared for their stand.

I found myself in a scene completely unlike the one I'd sketched in my teleportation diary.

The landscape was littered with armor—armor that had no doubt been worn by the undead horde before their bodies had faded away.

I also noticed an odd boulder in the middle of the plain. It looked almost like a small mountain had erupted out of the ground. Whatever happened here, the battle had clearly been intense, judging by the ravaged landscape.

Probably the biggest change of all was the massive crater that ran across the Wiel, just a short way off from the fort. Water was slowly filling the newly formed basin, creating a small pond.

"I can't believe... Well, actually, I suppose I *can* believe it."

There was only one person I knew who could completely transform the earth like this in such a short amount of time: Felfi Visrotte, the Dragon Lord.

Judging by the size of the crater, I figured she could've stood toe to toe with Archangel Savior Uriel, if not beat him outright. It absolutely blew my mind that beings like Felfi Visrotte even existed.

Looking closer, I saw that her attack hadn't just affected the enemy. The two forts where we'd stationed our troops had also suffered extensive damage to their outer walls. The stone bridge that had once spanned the river had also been reduced to rubble. It was pure chaos.

I looked around for the person—or dragon, rather—that had caused this damage.

"Kyii! Kyiiiii!"

Ponta drew my attention behind me. I turned to see the Dragon Lord approaching in her humanoid form. Her long, violet hair billowed in the wind.

"Well, fancy meeting you here! So, I guess that means you guys've finished things on your end too?"

I nodded. "I came to pick up Fangas, Margrave Brahniey, and Prince Sekt, so we can report on the Salma front to those back in Saureah. Do you know where they are?"

The Dragon Lord glanced from one fort to the other. She smirked as she spoke.

"Fangas and the Margrave are giving cleanup orders to their troops. Sekt suffered an injury and is resting."

Looking back over the cluttered battlefield, I could see that the enemy forces hadn't managed to inflict anywhere near the damage they'd done in Delfrent.

I wondered just how many casualties we'd suffered along the way. If Prince Sekt, the leader of the Rhoden forces, had been injured, that could greatly harm our unification efforts, which was something I wanted to avoid at all costs.

"Well then, I think I'll check in on Sekt and see if I can help him."

I figured I'd cast a healing spell on the prince and then on anyone else who was seriously injured. That should at least keep us from losing too many soldiers. I wouldn't have time to heal everyone right now, so those with lesser injuries would just have to tough it out the traditional way.

"I'll let the other two know you've arrived."

With that, Felfi Visrotte was off into the sky. I felt strange using a Dragon Lord as a messenger, but she seemed to want to do it, so who was I to stop her?

It was difficult to get a sense of Sekt's injuries just by looking at him, but he seemed to have suffered several broken bones. After casting Over Heal on him, though, he seemed to be fine.

His eyes went wide at how quickly his body healed, and he even smacked himself a few times to check for lingering pain, against the protests of his soldiers. The prince looked like a new man.

Sekt then asked me to heal a few dozen of his troops, a task I happily took on. Just as I was finishing that up, Fangas and Brahniey entered the fort.

The margrave offered a few words of praise as he entered the room.

"Ah, Arc. Felfi Visrotte told us we'd find you here. I hear you were able to clear out the Delfrent Kingdom with little trouble. Good on ya, lad."

Fangas hefted his mammoth hammer onto his shoulder and turned the subject to his granddaughter.

"How did Ariane and the others fare?"

Something told me that if I mentioned I'd almost wiped out his beloved granddaughter with a powerful magic attack, his hammer might very well find its way to my face, so I decided to gloss over that part.

"Ariane and Chiyome are still back in Lione, heading up the search for survivors."

Fangas nodded. "All right then. We'll leave the rest to our commanders. Brahniey and I will accompany you back to Saureah."

Prince Sekt wasn't too keen on this idea.

"Now wait just a moment. I should go too, as a representative of the Rhoden Kingdom."

It seemed like he was back to his normal self.

Fangas raised a skeptical eyebrow at the young prince. "If you insist, then so be it. Arc?"

"Got it."

Even though his injuries had been healed, it still would do some good for the Prince to rest up. Alas, it didn't seem like he was going to change his mind.

A few moments later, we were back in Saureah, the capital of the Nohzan Kingdom.

The faces in the castle's meeting room were decidedly brighter than they had been the last time we'd gathered. Princess Riel was practically beaming.

"You've already freed Delfrent?" King Asparuh asked in disbelief.

Dillan opted to keep his response vague. "Well, let's just say that our plan went a lot better than expected."

I could feel the village elder's eyes on me, but I kept my eyes fixed on the map laid out on the table.

Next to speak was Margrave Brahniey. He turned to Fangas and Dillan and bowed low before offering his report.

"We were able to hold the defensive line at Brahniey's border and destroy the invaders from the Holy Hilk

Kingdom. Felfi Visrotte's power truly defies all human understanding."

The Margrave ran a hand through his receding gray hair and let out a sigh of amazement.

The same thought had crossed my own mind. It was hard to put into words just how awe-inspiring it was to witness the immense power involved in creating a lake where there had only been an empty plain.

The people of this world were no strangers to the monsters roaming their lands, but the power wielded by the Dragon Lord was something else entirely—something more in the domain of gods or demons.

Were Ariane here, she would almost certainly have pointed out that I, too, was able to perform such feats, but I didn't feel like Felfi Visrotte and I were even remotely on the same level. While my Paladin class could inflict a great deal of damage, I was keenly aware of the fact that this was only because I was borrowing the power of the archangels.

I'd slowly come to acknowledge the immense power lurking within me, but I still didn't feel like I could take credit for it. Summoning Uriel had really driven this point home. Alas, I didn't feel like I could explain this feeling in words.

"...which means we should be free to move on the Holy Hilk Kingdom." Dillan's voice broke through my thoughts. He was pointing out landmarks on the map and discussing our next steps. "We'll teleport our forces to Fehrbio Alsus and strike at the capital."

This plan seemed to take the humans in the room by surprise. King Asparuh was the first to speak up.

"Now, let's just wait a moment. Yes, we agreed that the Holy Hilk Kingdom was next, and that hasn't changed, but attacking the capital directly without a proper strategy...that's something else entirely."

From what I could infer, his greatest concern was that if we were to invade a foreign country without properly securing supply lines, then we risked our armies becoming completely cut off.

But that only applied to normal armies.

"Your concerns are well-founded, King Asparuh. However, our plan is to teleport straight into the heart of the Holy Hilk Kingdom and deliver a decisive blow. Not only does this eliminate our need for dedicated supply lines, but we also won't need a direction to fall back in if we're routed. After all, we could easily return here if need be. Our goal is to take out the pontiff. That's all."

Dillan pointed to the black token sitting on the capital of the Holy Hilk Kingdom.

King Asparuh, Margrave Brahniey, and Prince Sekt

frowned at the map. They didn't seem convinced that this strategy would succeed.

Between the gifted elven soldiers, the speed at which this war was progressing, and my ability to teleport soldiers in and out of a battlefield at will, the human side of this equation didn't have much to contribute. This was beyond anything they'd ever experienced.

My power in particular was like being able to move any piece directly next to your opponent's king in chess.

And that was only taking the front-line troops into account. With the immense power the Dragon Lords harbored, it was like flipping the entire chess board over and playing with new rules made up on the fly.

Prince Sekt was the first to break the silence, a sly grin on his face. "I see no problem with a quick, decisive battle. I assume we can count on the Dragon Lords to join us?"

Dillan nodded. "Yes, we'll need their support. I'd like to limit the amount of time we have to keep our forces away from home."

King Asparuh agreed to this as well. But something still seemed to be bothering the margrave. After glaring at the spot on the map that marked Larisa in the Salma Kingdom, he looked up and addressed the room.

"I see no problem with your plan to attack the capital. However, I would like to ask for your assistance in liberating Larisa. From what you mentioned earlier, Arc, the capital is still occupied by the undead. If there are any survivors left within the city's walls, I want to rescue them as soon as possible."

While the capital of Delfrent was being cleared out, we'd only managed to hold the line at the Wiel River, the border between the Salma Kingdom proper and the Brahniey domain. With the bridge now out of service, it would take a considerable amount of time before he could send help.

Since I'd already sketched Larisa, I could teleport there anytime I wanted. Bringing a force large enough to secure the city wouldn't be much of a challenge.

Furthermore, it would probably do us a lot of good in the long run to liberate the capital of the Salma Kingdom.

Dillan thought this over for a moment. "Looking for undead can be hard work. Why don't we split the elven and Jinshin forces in Delfrent and send half of them to Larisa? I figure they should be able to clear out both cities in around two days. Then we can give them all a day to rest up."

Not needing to rely on sight alone, the elves and mountain people were especially well-suited to the task of tracking down and slaying any lingering undead. The same task would take far longer if the humans were to do it alone.

Everyone seemed to agree with Dillan's plan.

"All right then. Margrave, we'll move your forces stationed near the Wiel up to the capital and leave operational control to you. The survivors would probably be happier to see a fellow Brahniey leading them."

After a look around the room to check for consensus, the matter was settled, and everyone hurried off to begin their preparations.

I gazed out the window. In just three days' time, we'd be taking the fight to the Holy Hilk Kingdom and putting an end to this once and for all.

The vast sky above seemed utterly unconcerned with the huge losses suffered in the neighboring nations, nor the massive battle about to take place. No matter where, or even when, you happened to live, the sky was always the same, brilliant shade of blue.

CHAPTER 4

The Final Battle

THE HOLY HILK KINGDOM was one of a cluster of four countries located in the southwest region of the northern continent. It was also the land were the Hilk's most fervent believers gathered.

Even with the massive Great West Revlon Empire, one of the biggest countries on the entire continent, sitting along its northern border, the Holy Hilk Kingdom had been allowed to thrive with little outside interference. However, this had more to do with geography than politics.

The first major barrier was the massive Beek Sea that cut the southwest off from the rest of the northern continent. The towering Rutios Mountains provided another natural border to the northeast.

Mount Alsus, in the Rutios range, was heavily mined for mythril. At the base of this mountain lay the sprawling city of Fehrbio Alsus, the holy capital and center of the Hilk religion.

Prior to the pontiff taking control over the country, these lands had been known as the Holy Kingdom of Alsus. The city was called the Ancient Capital and had survived for generations, which meant its buildings had a rather distinct look.

In a world where human cities were often lost to monsters or melee, this served as a great source of pride for the city's residents. Over the same period, other cities had been lost to fires, disasters, and wars.

This had all changed once the Hilk took over, erecting churches throughout the city. These churches, and the Hilk faith, began to spread across the land, and the beautifully spartan houses of worship soon became a fixture in many cities.

The Hilk's church-building techniques had been refined over the years in Fehrbio Alsus. Residents could look back through time just by walking the city streets.

At the center of the Ancient Capital stood a particularly majestic building, which towered over those around it. This was the cathedral, where all the faithful in the capital gathered.

This immense church and its bell towers could be easily seen even from beyond the outer walls, and it served as an awe-inspiring sight to all who approached Fehrbio Alsus.

And yet, despite the city's beauty, many of its buildings had fallen into disrepair, with some reduced to little more than rubble. Its streets were a mere shadow of their former selves.

What had once served as the vibrant capital of the Hilk religion was now devoid of people; a proverbial ghost town.

Amid this oppressive silence, however, was a sight that defied explanation: towering monsters standing nearly fifty meters tall, walking among the buildings like children stomping around a toy town. Giants might be the first word to come to mind, though these massive creatures made the so-called giants on the southern continent look like dwarves.

When I saw them, I couldn't believe my eyes. These abominations looked like they were made up of human bodies strung together in one large mass, reminding me of Cardinal Charros's monster form.

The most likely explanation was that the city's residents had been used to create these creatures. Exactly *how* they'd come to serve as fodder for the giants was unclear, but as long as there was the possibility of survivors within the city limits, it would be best to keep destruction to a minimum.

I was floored by the pontiff's ability to create such huge beings on a whim. The two days we'd dedicated to liberating Larisa had probably given him the time he needed, but there was no sense in dwelling on that now.

Fehrbio Alsus had fallen, and there was no going back.

The Brahniey forces, elves, and members of the Jinshin clan had done well to clear out Larisa under the margrave's leadership, while rescue operations were conducted concurrently in Lione.

Despite our best efforts, we found few survivors in Lione. We had greater success in Larisa, where more of the populace had been able to escape.

According to the margrave's report, less than a third of the city's original population remained.

The number of survivors led to a new problem, however: arguments of control and succession among the surviving nobility. But the margrave was having none of it and immediately placed himself in provisional control of the kingdom. With the elven and Jinshin forces behind him, there wasn't much room for argument.

There was the risk, however, that those not fond of the margrave might stage a coup, now that we'd moved the soldiers out of Larisa for our assault on the Holy Hilk Kingdom. To minimize this, Dillan had left 1,000 elven soldiers behind to supplement the margrave's forces and maintain order.

I couldn't help but appreciate the irony that controlling a free city was infinitely more challenging than liberating an occupied one. At the end of the day, humans were their own greatest enemy.

Just as Dillan had predicted, we only needed two days in Larisa. We then gave the soldiers a day to rest while I left with Felfi Visrotte for the Holy Hilk Kingdom to find a good teleportation spot and gather some intelligence on our enemies.

The first time we'd visited, these giants hadn't been here.

I had no idea just how powerful the leader of the Hilk actually was, but I had a hard time believing that he could create such immense creatures in a day. Otherwise, he would have done the same back in the Delfrent Kingdom to bolster his forces.

This could only mean one thing...

When I'd come here to find a good teleportation point, I'd had Felfi Visrotte drop me a fair distance away from the capital, and I'd teleported my way in using Dimensional Step to make sure that the pontiff didn't see me coming.

This meant that my view had been obscured by the countless undead wandering around the outskirts of the capital, not to mention the protective walls surrounding it, preventing me from getting a good look at what was going on inside.

The giants must have been underground at that time, or were somehow hidden from view.

"Never in all my years have I seen such disgusting creatures," Felfi Visrotte growled as she gazed at the giants. We were currently flying around the city to get a look at our objective before the upcoming assault.

Dragon Lords hated undead to their very core, and the giants below seemed to bother her even more.

From a distance, the creatures looked as if they were covered in inflamed skin. They stood in place, watching our every movement.

Their eyes and mouths—or the spots where these would have been on a normal person—were large, hollowed out cavities, and their faces were completely devoid of any expression. It was...unsettling.

"They're just...watching us."

"Kyii! Kyiiiii!"

Ponta offered its own attempt at a menacing threat to the monsters below.

"I'd love to get a closer look, but since we don't know what kind of abilities those things can bring to bear, it's probably best to keep our distance."

It didn't look like we'd learn a whole lot more just by circling around, so I figured it best that we turn back. To my surprise, Felfi Visrotte began descending instead.

"Well, we'll just have to find out, then. Hang on!"

She left no room for debate as she dropped down toward one of the giants. It seemed to grow bigger as we drew close.

The giant's face locked onto us, firing a massive black ball out of the hole where its mouth should have been.

BWAFOOM!!!

"Wha?!"

The blast shook the air like a thunderclap as the black ball barreled toward us.

Felfi Visrotte deftly dodged the incoming object, and I turned to watch it crash into the ground, far in the distance. The black substance quickly melted away, eroding everything it touched.

I shuddered at the thought of what it could do to me. Felfi Visrotte seemed to share my concerns.

"I've never heard of death contamination being used as a weapon like this!"

This "death contamination" was a unique aura that emanated from the undead. Though I couldn't see it myself, elves were able to use it to tell if someone was undead or not. But this thing the giant had shot at us was a physical sphere.

The only way I could explain it was that the death contamination within the sphere was far denser than usual, which allowed me to see it.

"Kyi! Kyii!" Ponta called out a warning from where it was wrapped around my neck.

I turned back just in time to see the giant slowly twist its massive body, its feet tearing up the streets below as it shifted, and fire another volley. There were three projectiles this time.

BWAFOOM!!! BWAFOOM!!! BWAFOOM!!!

Felfi Visrotte spun, gracefully dodging this barrage as well.

Unfortunately, I wasn't quite so lucky. I lost my grip on her back and fell.

"Hyaaaaaaaaaaaaaaaaaaaaaaaaaauuugh!!!"

"Kyiiiiiiiiiiiiiiii!!!"

I was helpless as my body spun end over end, the ground rushing up to meet me. After a bit of effort, I managed to straighten myself out and started looking for a place on the ground to teleport to.

However, at the rate I was falling, it was hard to focus on any specific landmark. The ground was rapidly approaching, and I was running out of options. I searched desperately for something, anything, to latch onto. Just as I was about to hit the ground, I felt an incredible force slam into my side, catching me. Looking up, I met Felfi Visrotte's reptilian gaze.

"Sorry 'bout that, Arc. Anyway, just try to hang on a bit longer while I get us back to the rest of the army."

She'd caught me right in her massive jaws. From an outsider's perspective, it must've looked like she was eating me.

While I was happy not to have fallen to my death, we were hardly out of the woods yet.

The two giants were now working in concert to coordinate their attacks on Felfi Visrotte and block her escape. The battle had only grown more intense.

For her part, the Dragon Lord shot off several energy blasts at the giants in an attempt to overwhelm them. The attacks looked similar to the one she'd used against me back at the stadium.

The energy blasted away chunks of the giants upon impact, but the holes quickly filled with more human parts. Apparently, they had the ability to regenerate too.

Felfi Visrotte's attacks on the black spheres, however, fared a bit better. She was able to blast the incoming shots right out of the sky, though she was having a hard time keeping up with the incoming barrage.

As she weaved through several more shots, I noticed one more coming straight for us. Without thinking, I cast a spell.

"Holy Protection!"

A bright light began spreading out from me and across Felfi Visrotte's body, like a thin, glowing membrane surrounding us.

The black sphere struck her side only a moment later, exploding in a black mist that quickly dissipated.

The two giants slowed their movements, giving Felfi Visrotte a chance to finally put some distance between us and them.

Once we were out of range of their attacks, they immediately stopped shooting.

I glanced down at the giants and the streets torn up beneath them. If there had been anyone left alive in those piles of rubble, they were almost certainly dead now.

The Dragon Lord turned to look at me. "Thanks for the assist back there, Arc."

Holy Protection was a support ability from the Paladin class that shielded you and your party members from dark-elemental attacks. It seemed to have worked perfectly. Unfortunately, the spell had worn off after the blow, and her body had returned to normal.

I risked another glance down from my perch. The two giants were following us intently with the caverns that served as their eyes.

Without a doubt, they would prove to be a major

obstacle in our assault on Alsus. I could only imagine what would happen to the rank-and-file soldiers if they were hit by one of those black spheres.

Felfi Visrotte glowered at the disgusting creatures below and offered a plan of her own. "Do you think if Villy and I draw those disgusting beasts' attention, you could take down the person behind all this?"

I'd completely forgotten that we had another Dragon Lord at our disposal.

I'd originally been thinking of facing the giants using my Paladin abilities, but that would present a great risk to the two Dragon Lords if they also joined in the battle. Besides, I had serious doubts about whether I'd actually be able to take those two on by myself, especially if I hoped to leave any of the city intact.

I agreed to Felfi Visrotte's plan and asked her to take me back to the outskirts, where the rest of our forces were waiting.

She beat her massive wings to pick up speed. I leaned back, trying to enjoy the ride while I thought about the upcoming battle.

I crossed my arms and groaned. There was also the fact that the pontiff was nowhere to be found. But would he really have left his entire kingdom behind?

I didn't know a whole lot about his personality, so it

was possible that he'd abandoned the city. However, I had a hard time believing that he'd just leave these...things.

Either way, we needed to purge the undead from the Hilk capital.

We arrived at the location to the southeast of Fehrbio Alsus where the rest of our forces were waiting. I was still hanging out of Felfi Visrotte's mouth.

Ten thousand troops had gathered here, of different species and nations: humans from the Nohzan Kingdom, the Rhoden Kingdom, and Brahniey in the Salma Kingdom; elves from Maple and Drant; mountain people from the Jinshin clan; and two Dragon Lords. It truly was a sight to behold.

This was probably the first time in history that so many people of different species and creeds had come together. This was evident in the way they watched each other with great interest.

In the middle of this patchwork sat a large tent where all the commanders of the different forces met to discuss strategy.

I stood in the center of the tent, all eyes on me.

Dillan furrowed his brow. "Indestructible giants? I never would have imagined they'd have such things."

Ariane stood at her father's side, her face taut with concern.

Fangas, the muscle-bound high elder from the Great Canada Forest, spoke next. "And what about those dense balls of death contamination? If someone got hit by one, they'd be dead before they knew what happened. Judging from the sheer size of the things, their range must be pretty impressive. I don't even know how we'll approach the capital, let alone take it back."

Upon hearing about the death contamination spheres shot by the undead giants, everyone in the room had grown visibly tense.

There was only one person smiling throughout all of this: Felfi Visrotte. She stood next to me in her humanoid form, confidence radiating from her face.

"Now, don't you worry. Villiers Fim and I will keep those giants busy for ya. Besides, Arc here can cast a spell on y'all that will protect you from one—but only one—of those death contamination shots. That makes it at least a little better, now doesn't it?"

With that, all eyes were back on me.

Margrave Brahniey was the first to question this. "Is that true, Arc?"

I mean, sure, I'd only just discovered that this spell even worked, but I didn't need to tell *them* that.

"I used it on Felfi Visrotte earlier, and despite taking a direct hit, we survived without suffering any ill effects.

However, it remains to be seen whether the human body can survive a direct hit, even with Holy Protection to absorb the death contamination."

Sure, a powerful creature like a Dragon Lord could withstand it, but a normal human might just get blown away. Casting Holy Protection on the troops was no guarantee that they'd be safe.

Prince Sekt, leader of the Rhoden forces, brushed his bangs out of his eyes and sighed.

"Well, I imagine the easiest way to minimize the risk to our forces is to avoid any large formations. That way we don't lose a bunch of soldiers all in one go." From his sardonic grin, it was clear that he'd suffered no lasting effects from his previous injuries.

Next to speak was Zahar Bakharov, Princess Riel's bodyguard and the man commanding the Nohzan army. "That would mean organizing our troops into small squads to carry out guerrilla strikes, but I don't know how much good even that will do us. So long as those giants are around, I don't think we stand a chance at assaulting the capital."

At the request of King Asparuh himself, Niena, Riel's other bodyguard, was serving as Zahar's advisor. What the two of them lacked in authority and political influence, they more than made up for in experience. They were slowly gaining more esteem in the King's eyes.

Chiyome, one of the six great warriors of the Jinshin clan, and the youngest person in the room, chimed in next. "We need to remember that we aren't fighting another army of humans, but disorganized undead forces without any real sense of strategy. I think it would be best for us to wait until the giants are preoccupied with the Dragon Lords and then draw the undead out into the open to attack them in small groups. All while staying out of the giants' range, of course."

Goemon, the hulking feline who could even put the muscular Fangas to shame, crossed his arms and nodded in agreement with his younger companion.

It would be easy to discount Chiyome due to her diminutive size, but the mammoth cat man standing behind her lent additional weight to her words. Not that it was needed; most of the people in this tent were well aware of her abilities.

The only one who surprised me was Prince Sekt. I'd originally written him off as just another young royal, but he'd proven himself in the battle over the Wiel River, personally leading the charge into swarming undead.

Now that we'd gained some consensus, Dillan offered an impassioned speech. "I think that's an excellent idea, Chiyome. I would like each of the forces to formulate their own strategy around this plan. Remember, everyone, this will be our last battle with the Holy Hilk Kingdom. Once this matter has been resolved, we will begin a new chapter in our shared history. We are standing at the cusp of a brand-new future for all of us."

After letting out a small cheer, the leaders immediately left the tent and hurried back to their respective forces to pass along the marching orders.

"Well, it looks like the battle is about to start."

"Kyii!"

I reached down and patted the spirit creature wrapped around my neck as I stepped out of the tent. I could just barely make out the outline of the massive cathedral of Fehrbio Alsus to the northeast.

Beside me were Ariane, with her hair tied back in a ponytail, and Chiyome, who'd redone her hair with a ribbon—black, to match her clothes. Goemon approached and bumped my fist in greeting before turning to look at the capital as well.

"Well, I guess we should get going?"

"Yeah."

"Guess so."

"Hm."

It looked like we were all in agreement.

Felfi Visrotte arched her neck to look at Arc and all the soldiers gathered together in the distance.

"Looks like they're about to start, yeah?"

She spread her beautiful, violet-patterned wings as far as they would go, then flapped them a few times, as if to make sure they were still working. Even that simple act kicked up a violent gust of wind.

Compared to his fellow Dragon Lord, Villiers Fim sounded far less confident as he gazed at Arc and the others. "Shouldn't we get going soon?"

For a moment, Felfi Visrotte looked taken aback by this. Then she opened her mouth wide and cackled. "And here I thought your heart wasn't in the fight, boy. Now look at you, all ready to go."

Villiers Fim scowled and averted his gaze, twisting his large tail around to scratch the back of his neck. "I was just thinking about how things will settle down a bit once we get this out of the way. That's all."

Felfi Visrotte let out another loud, throaty laugh. "Fine, fine. Let's be off then, yeah?"

With another powerful thrust of her wings, she was airborne.

From the sky, the army of 10,000 looked disjointed, the soldiers all operating in small, independent squads as they marched toward the same goal: the holy capital.

Any moment now, the forces below would stop just shy of the giants' attack range.

Felfi Visrotte tried to spot Arc in the crowd. Thanks to her excellent vision, she found him among the other infantry in no time. She picked up speed, Villiers Fim following close behind. A moment later, the two Dragon Lords landed right in front of him.

"Holy Protection!" Arc cast the spell as soon as they came to a stop.

Glowing light surrounded their bodies as the magic took effect. Felfi Visrotte gave herself a quick once-over, then she was airborne again, heading for the capital. Villiers Fim followed soon after.

The closer they drew to the capital, the more undead they saw amassing outside the city limits.

"Take some of this!"

Felfi Visrotte let off a volley of glowing projectiles flying down to the earth like shooting stars. They exploded with a massive roar, sending dirt and limbs everywhere.

Arc had referred to this as an "aerial bombing."

"Gyahaha! Like music to my ears!"

As the Dragon Lord took a victory lap after her devastating attack, she summoned hundreds of tiny balls of light around her body, then sent them down on the enemy troops as well.

Though each of the individual blasts was much weaker compared to the previous attack, they more than made up for it in sheer density, blanketing the land in fiery death.

Not wanting to be left out, Villiers Fim released a massive tornado of his own, which tore across the plains, leaving a trail of carnage in its wake. The whole affair was about as strenuous to the Dragon Lords as mowing a somewhat unwieldy lawn.

Alas, their fun ended once the giants at the center of the capital caught sight of them and started shooting black spheres of death contamination. It was time to get serious.

Their emotionless, gaping maws of raw flesh followed the Dragon Lords as they approached, shooting sphere after sphere in an attempt to hit their targets.

As each black sphere smashed into the earth, they melted into a disgusting corrosive substance that disintegrated everything they touched...even the undead.

The Dragon Lords split up, still dodging the incoming shots. Within minutes, they'd reached the city limits and were within range of the protective wall surrounding the capital. Felfi Visrotte opened her mouth, accumulating energy into a massive ball of light, which she shot at the wall below.

With a flash and a thunderous boom, a massive gash

was torn into the wall. Its integrity compromised, the wall began crumbling, like an avalanche of stone.

Villiers Fim passed into the capital proper, dodging shots as he closed in on the giants. One of them reached for him, but was quickly knocked back, thanks to another blast from Felfi Visrotte.

The attack might have struck the giant's arm off were it not for its fast-acting regenerative abilities. Flesh and muscle bubbled out from within, reconnecting the limb almost immediately.

Felfi Visrotte was now thoroughly enraged. "These are gonna be a real pain in the ass! Can't you just die already, your sick freaks?!"

She swooped in close and swung her dagger-like tail into the giant's face, lopping off the top half of its head.

The giant shuddered, and it seemed as if its entire body screamed in unison. A black mist rose off its body as it frantically searched for the rest of its head. However, Felfi Visrotte was the first to find it and shot multiple blasts at the severed flesh, blowing it to oblivion.

The giant turned its attention back to her and launched another barrage of the black spheres. She ducked behind a building for cover before launching higher into the air. She retreated, putting some distance between her and the monster.

"You're really startin' to annoy me, y'know? I don't feel like playing this game all day."

She launched another volley, watching as each ball of energy exploded with an enormous blast that sent pieces of flesh flying in every direction. The immense giant stumbled.

The Dragon Lord pressed her assault as she pushed closer, swinging her razor-sharp tail into the giant's right arm, followed by its left, cleanly lopping off both of them.

The giant fell to its knees, casting about for its missing limbs.

Felfi Visrotte launched another salvo at the severed arms, leaving nothing but dust behind. The giant now looked significantly weakened.

"You're way too big for your own good, boy. And I'm gonna fix that!"

Deftly dodging another round of black spheres, the Dragon Lord glanced over to check on Villiers Fim. She found him sending tornado after tornado at his own opponent, the powerful wind funnels surrounding the giant and pinning it in place.

Once it was stuck, Villiers Fim began shooting wind blades, chipping away at the giant's body like an artist carving ice.

Despite the undead giant's best efforts to regenerate, it was losing more and more mass by the minute. To Felfi

Visrotte's eye, it now looked a fair bit shorter than the giant she was facing.

Even though Villiers Fim couldn't bring anywhere near as much raw power to the battlefield as Felfi Visrotte could, he more than made up for it with his skill, as evidenced by this sustained attack.

The thousands of victims making up this giant let out an unsettling scream as the Dragon Lord chipped away at them, though their voices could only be faintly heard above the howling wind. Within minutes, the giant had been reduced to practically nothing.

Remembering that her own foe was still far from defeated, Felfi Visrotte turned to find that the armless giant was closing in on Villiers Fim.

"Oh, no!"

She flapped her wings in a desperate attempt to catch up.

The giant was practically on top of Villiers Fim when it launched its next volley of black spheres. Fortunately, he was able to blast them away with tornadoes.

The other giant took this opportunity to launch an attack of its own from within its wind prison. Villiers Fim lost focus, and his magic weakened, as he tried dodging the attacks from both directions. The confined giant used this opportunity to slam its body straight through the cyclones and break out.

Felfi Visrotte was furious with herself for having let her guard down like that, but there was no time to dwell on her mistake. She needed to take down the armlessgiant.

She dove for its back, where, much to her horror, a gaping hole opened, out of which shot another massive black sphere. It was coming right at her.

"Wha?!"

The sphere struck Felfi Visrotte in the head, knocking her back into a building. Thankfully, the magic spell Arc had cast on her earlier protected her from any of its ill effects.

The giant followed this up with a kick, which the Dragon Lord blocked with her tail. This stunned the giant just long enough to allow her to escape.

"If it weren't for Arc, I'd be a goner. I need to keep my guard up and remember that this monstrosity's face is nothing more than a decoration."

The giant shot several more black spheres out of its mouth, but they were no match for Felfi Visrotte's speed and agility. She returned the attacks blow for blow with energy blasts of her own.

While this was happening, Villiers Fim was slowly pulling back to gain some distance from his opponent.

The sky grew dark, and a bright flash of lighting struck the top of the giant's head, followed by an ear-shattering thunderclap. The corpses forming the surface of the giant's body were charred instantly, though even that damage was quickly regenerated.

"I've made some progress, but this is really starting to annoy me!"

The Dragon Lord launched several more tornadoes to knock his opponent's latest barrage off course before jerking to the side to avoid yet another attack from the armless giant.

This battle was taking a heavy toll on the capital, but the Dragon Lords didn't have the luxury of thinking about property damage at the moment.

Felfi Visrotte and Villiers Fim flew back again to get some breathing room, both launching attacks to keep the creatures at bay.

However, the giants completely ignored the barrage and pressed on, shooting sphere after sphere of death contamination. Felfi Visrotte grumbled deep in her throat. It began to feel as though the tables were turning—and not in the right direction.

All of a sudden, the armless giant and its shrunken comrade dove into each other. Within seconds, their bodies began melding.

"What?!"

"No way!"

The two giants morphed together, the corpses making up their bodies pooling and fusing. The single creature now had four arms, each with its own hole to shoot more black spheres. Combined with the one in its face, it could now launch five projectiles at once.

"C'mon, give us a break! This is getting ridiculous!"

Felfi Visrotte shot a volley of energy blasts to destroy some of the incoming spheres, while pulling off impressive aerobatic maneuvers to avoid the ones she couldn't hit.

The monster continued growing, angling its upper body and launching black spheres like it was some sort of anti-aircraft artillery. Felfi Visrotte swooped through the barrage until she was within striking distance and slashed clean through one of its arms with her tail. However, the giant simply stomped on its own severed arm, absorbing the mass of flesh into its leg. A moment later, a new arm emerged.

Villiers Fim sent a fusillade of wind blades at their enlarged opponent, but it regenerated just as fast as either of them could damage it.

The giant was now standing at an impressive ninety meters tall—larger even than Felfi Visrotte, and more than double the size of Villiers Fim.

"Gyaugh! Its regeneration speed has increased too!"

Villiers Fim dodged another shot and decided to fall back to get some breathing room.

Suddenly, each of the giant's four arms split in half, giving it eight cannons to shoot from. This kept Felfi Visrotte from getting too close, her only option now to attack from above with her energy blasts. But with each successful blow, the giant simply stomped on any severed body part and reabsorbed it.

Felfi Visrotte was starting to reach her limit. Out of frustration, she was considering simply blasting away the ground itself when her thoughts were suddenly interrupted. The giant's foot began glowing.

Once again, the corpses making up the massive creature began shrieking in unison, as if the door to hell had been opened, unleashing the screams of the damned.

When the light faded, she saw that the giant was now standing on just one leg, the other having completely vanished below the knee. It lost its balance and tumbled forward.

The giant hit the ground with such force that the shockwave alone leveled all of the nearby buildings. A massive cloud of dust kicked up, obscuring the central capital.

The Dragon Lords weren't about to let such a perfect opportunity go to waste. Even through the thick dust, they were still able to pick out their target; such were their keenly tuned senses for hunting the undead.

"You can't hide from me that easily!"

Felfi Visrotte dove down into the dense dust and chopped off two of the giant's arms, then shot back up into the sky. Villiers Fim sent out two more tornado blasts to tear the arms to shreds before they could regenerate, leaving chunks no larger than a pebble in their place.

"Looks like we just might win yet!"

Felfi Visrotte let out a hearty chuckle as she launched back into the dust cloud to inflict more wounds. With every piece of flesh she lopped off, Villiers Fim would follow up with his powerful wind bursts to destroy it.

They repeated this process over and over until the haunted screams of the dead fell silent, only to be replaced by the Dragon Lords' roar of victory.

As the armies approached Fehrbio Alsus's outer wall, the bell towers of the massive cathedral seemed to double in size. The closer they got, the more undead remains they encountered, completely annihilated by the thick, black contamination of death.

The army had split into small units, careful to maintain

distance from one another as they advanced on the capital. Each and every soldier was on alert for any hidden undead. Though this abundance of caution was necessary, it made for very slow progress.

The entire formation was led by Ariane and a group of elves, Chiyome and a contingent of the Jinshin clan, and a group of human knights.

Arc marched cheerfully at the front, stroking the spirit creature wrapped tightly around his neck.

Fangas looked over at his granddaughter, who'd been silently staring at Arc's back. "You nervous, Ariane?"

He was about as tall and muscular as Arc, and wore tight-fitting leather armor pocked with battle scars. According to the stories she'd heard, her grandfather had singlehandedly taken down a cardinal on the front lines of the Wiel, using the massive war hammer he carried on his back.

Though it'd been ages since he'd retired from military service, the years didn't seem to have slowed him one bit.

Ariane sighed. "A little, I guess. I mean, with all those undead out there waiting for us..."

Chiyome turned to Ariane and raised a fist, determined to cheer her up. "Don't worry, Ariane! I'll keep you safe!"

Ariane felt herself flush. She gave her cheeks a gentle slap to focus herself.

Fangas looked down at his granddaughter and rapped his fist against the thick armor covering his chest. "Thinking too much leads to paralysis. Besides, I'm here. Now's your chance to show me what you're made of."

He flashed a broad, toothy grin, though the scar running down his face still lent him an intimidating air.

Ariane gave a determined nod and focused her attention ahead.

A few moments later, the sound of massive wings flapping filled the air. The two Dragon Lords swooped down and landed in front of Arc.

Things were going exactly as planned.

Arc raised his right fist high into the air and cast a spell. "Holy Protection!"

A bright flash of light spread out from him until it encompassed the mammoth Dragon Lords, Ariane, Chiyome, Fangas, Goemon, and all the other soldiers nearby. Once cast, a thin layer of light surrounded their bodies.

This display of magic shocked the humans, of course, but even the elves seemed surprised by the scale of this particular spell.

As Arc explained it, the spell would protect them from the toxic effects of the giants' death contamination, though the effect would only last for a single blow.

The Dragon Lords took to the air again, heading straight for the capital. Moments later, Felfi Visrotte began shooting blasts of light down at the ground, sending plumes of dirt and smoke high into the air.

Even at this distance, Ariane and Chiyome could feel the ground beneath them shake as the pressure waves rocked the earth.

Villiers Fim flew behind and slightly to the side of his larger companion, loosing tornado blasts that threw anyone in their path high into the sky.

Their devastating assault cleared a route from the army all the way to the gates of the capital. Once the soldiers realized what the Dragon Lords had done, they erupted into boisterous cheers.

While the troops celebrated their good fortune, Arc used Dimensional Step to teleport to the remaining squads, stopping just long enough to cast Holy Protection on them.

It was time for the united forces to march on the capital.

One of the human squads rushed ahead to take down some of the weakened undead that the Dragon Lords had missed. They met little resistance, which only served to spur them on to find more enemies to fight.

However, they soon ran into a man-spider with half of its upper body missing. It clawed up from the rubble, its remaining hands clutching a massive sword. By the time the frenzied soldiers caught sight of it, it was too late.

"Watch out!" One of the soldiers let out a shrill scream.

They suddenly realized just how exposed they were and started running toward the relative safety of the front lines.

"F-fall back!!!" Another soldier barked commands in an attempt to get the rest under some semblance of order.

The man-spider rushed ahead, swinging its giant blade, the stump of its missing human torso flapping loosely behind it.

The soldiers screamed and howled as they came to terms with their imminent death. Suddenly, a voice broke through the pandemonium.

"Savage Spike!"

By the time these words reached the soldier's ears, a single arrow was already sticking out of the man-spider's remaining torso. Then, a moment later...

BASHOOM!

The man-spider's upper body was torn apart in a violent explosion. Its spider legs took another two or three steps before collapsing, motionless, before fizzling away into a black sludge.

The soldiers' ears were still ringing as they searched for whoever had come to their aid. They spotted a single elf nearby, bow at the ready. She humbly acknowledged their thanks with a simple nod of her head.

However, her magical arrow only marked the beginning of the barrage. As if on cue, the rest of the elven archers let their arrows fly. They passed over the human soldiers' heads to impale more man-spiders off in the distance. Just like before, there was a brief pause followed by a thunderous boom. The serenity that had once lay over this field was a distant memory.

The elves usually reserved such magical arrow attacks for the largest monsters that roamed the Great Canada Forest, usually in order to ensure a hit through dense vegetation.

But since the attack was powerful enough to rip someone clean in half, it was the perfect choice to use against the man-spiders.

During the planning phase, it had been decided that the elves, with their impressive array of magical techniques, and the physically gifted Jinshin clan would focus on clearing out the man-spiders, while the humans focused on slaying the undead infantry.

Prince Sekt led the Rhoden troops in several separate but tightly integrated squads. The advance guard consisted of infantry carrying tower shields, which created an impenetrable moving wall. While the undead occupied themselves with the shield bearers, the soldiers behind skewered the enemy with spears.

Though this greatly slowed their advance, it also meant that all the undead in their way were completely annihilated, clearing a path for the elven archers to follow.

Of course, they were only able to operate like this as long as they stayed outside the range of the undead giants.

In the distance, a trumpet sounded, causing Margrave Brahniey to groan. The nearby elves, who weren't used to fighting in large-scale conflicts like this, grew visibly confused at this sudden noise.

Unlike the soldiers serving under Prince Sekt, the margrave's commanders expertly led their squads without additional orders. Such was the breadth of their training. They linked up with and separated from other squads as needed, like a well-oiled machine.

It had also become clear that Zahar—the leader of the Nohzan forces, supported by Niena—had little experience in large-scale troop movements. There was hardly any cohesion between his squads.

However, the sight of Zahar rushing ahead and cleaving any enemy that crossed his path did a lot for the soldiers' morale. After all, he'd come up from the same humble beginnings as them.

Though the unified forces could only muster around

10,000 soldiers, they were still able to hold their own against the legions of undead, thanks to the Dragon Lords, who'd forced the enemy to spread out.

And then there was the other heavy damage dealer up front, breaking up any undead clusters.

"Lightning Damper!"

Arc had charged into the heart of the enemy and let loose a powerful area-of-effect spell that sent lightning bolts raining from the sky.

He them teleported into another cluster and used a different technique.

"Bring Whirlwind!"

This attack caused a powerful gust of air to whip around, lifting the undead high into the air before dumping them unceremoniously on the ground, where they were quickly dispatched by the advancing troops.

Even after casting so many spells, Arc didn't look winded. He was proving himself an invaluable ally on the battlefield.

The elves who'd watched his match against Felfi Visrotte back in the Maple stadium cheered him on as he tore through the enemy. They had high expectations for him, and he didn't disappoint.

Ariane glowered at Arc as she struck down undead on her own. "Well, I'm not about to let him hog all the attention!"

She reached her free hand into her bag and pulled out a tubular object.

"Spirits of fire, lend your ears and grant me your protection!"

A barrier of leaves materialized, protecting her. She swung her sword, and it burst into flames. She then held the tubular object in front of her and cleaved it in two with her burning blade. Flames poured out of it, further fueling her sword until the flames licking off it reached well into the sky. It almost looked as if she were wielding a bonfire.

"May your flames of retribution set those who have strayed back onto the proper path, ready to receive your guidance."

Dropping the rest of the tube, Ariane clasped the hilt of her sword firmly in both hands and lifted it high into the air, bathing everything around her in its flickering, red glow. She took a step forward and swung the blade with all her might, unleashing a massive pillar of fire.

The undead in its path were instantly reduced to ash.

The pillar of fire began transforming, growing flaming branches and even leaves.

Ariane smiled at the sight.

"I'm not holding back today! I've been granted permission to use powdered mana, so I'm free to show Arc a thing or two!"

Ariane reached into her bag again and pulled out another tube filled with powdered mana. While typically used as a power source for magical items, powdered mana was also used by elven soldiers to consume less of their spirit magic when casting spells.

It all sounded rather simple, but it took years of training to learn how to use powdered mana properly and in the right amounts, a skill that many battle-hardened veterans hadn't mastered.

After spending years watching her older sister, Eevin, use powdered mana expertly, Ariane began to see her own lack of skill as a personal shortcoming. Eventually, however, she'd realized that her sister simply stood a head above the rest, and there was no sense measuring herself against her sister. But that hadn't stopped Ariane from becoming an exceptional soldier in her own right.

Ariane's fellow elves watched in amazement as she used her powerful technique to incinerate swarms of undead.

Fangas looked especially proud of his granddaughter, even as he barreled his way through enemy soldiers, swinging his mammoth war hammer as if it weighed nothing.

"I'm not ceding my place to the next generation just yet!"

He offered a toothy grin and raised his hammer high.

"Great spirits of the earth, heed my call and offer me your protection!"

Leaves whipped up from the ground, forming a protective barrier around Fangas. Though this attack was incredibly similar to the one cast moments ago by Ariane, the energy radiating off his war hammer was something else entirely.

The air around the hammer shimmered as the ground beneath his feet groaned. Beams of light shot out of both the weapon and the earth, the energy accumulating at the hammer's head.

"Spirits, I summon you from your earthen slumber!"

The earth began shaking even more violently, as if something were clawing its way out of the planet's crust. The tremor was so violent that both enemy and ally alike struggled to stand.

"Spirits of the earth, call upon your wayward children and lead them back to the everlasting darkness!"

Fangas swung the massive hammer down, smashing the ground with such force that the earth itself tore open. The rift continued growing wider and wider into a dark, bottomless chasm that bore a disturbing resemblance to the mouth of a giant beast. Humans and elves alike watched, terrified, as it began swallowing the undead. Even the man-spiders weren't fast enough to outrun it.

After gorging itself on a significant number of the undead, the large mouth slowly closed, until there was no evidence that it had ever even existed.

"My friend here has been without its rune stone for far too long. It sure feels good to use it again." Fangas patted the head of his war hammer affectionately.

His hammer had been custom-built to store powdered mana within it, allowing him to use magical attacks on a whim. Though similar to the method used by Ariane, his attacks were far more destructive, on par with something Arc or even one of the Dragon Lords might pull off.

Throughout his life, Fangas had diligently collected the rune stones from each and every monster he'd killed and refined them into powdered mana. He'd then embedded this within his hammer so it would always be available to him.

Years had passed without an opportunity to use all of this hard-won powdered mana. In fact, Fangas had begun to wonder if perhaps his hammer was destined to become a decoration, its mana forever unused. It felt good to finally lay that question to rest.

He'd originally intended to use this specific attack during the battle over the Wiel, but after Felfi Visrotte had wiped out almost the entire invading army, using such power against the few remaining undead seemed like a waste.

Fangas rested the hammer against his shoulder and turned off his attention toward the capital. The two Dragon Lords were in a desperate battle against the giants towering over the city center. The unmitigated destruction was impossible to put into words.

On her way into the capital, Felfi Visrotte had blown a massive hole in the protective wall surrounding it, and the rest of the wall had crumbled in an avalanche of bricks.

Thanks to the sheer destructive force of the Dragon Lord's attack, as well as Fangas's powerful spirit magic, the route to the capital was now mostly clear, shy of some undead still trapped in the rubble.

The battle between the Dragon Lords and the giants was well and truly underway, with the mammoth monsters shooting spheres of death in every direction as the Dragon Lords closed in.

Fangas was relieved to see that the giants were too preoccupied with the Dragon Lords to pay much attention to the advancing foot soldiers. He couldn't bear to think about what would happen if they were hit by one of the death contamination projectiles.

The spheres were so massive that if the giants were to shoot one toward the troops in the field, there'd be nowhere for them to hide.

However, once they were within the city limits, there should be enough buildings to provide ample cover from any attacks the giants might send their way. Getting through the hole in the wall and into the city proper before they were spotted was of the utmost importance.

Fangas's voice boomed across the plains. "We've broken through! Follow me to the capital!" He charged, using his war hammer to bat enemy soldiers out of his way.

The elven soldiers responded with a battle cry and followed the high elder, killing any undead in their path.

The Jinshin clan, having helped the elves eliminate the man-spiders, responded next. Chiyome and Goemon led the group toward the shattered wall at such speed that they managed to overtake the elves.

"Body to earth, exploding steel fist!" Goemon clanked his metal gauntlets, and his arms grew hard, taking on a dull, silver sheen.

His fists dealt lethal blows to each undead enemy that came near, leaving a trail of crushed bodies in his wake.

"Body to water, aqua lance slash!"

Meanwhile, Chiyome used her water lance to perform deliberate, surgical strikes on her enemies, disarming them so that the troops behind her could pick them off.

Whether in a forest, on a plain, or even the middle of a wasteland, no one could match the pace of the Jinshin clan. They reached the outer wall far ahead of the rest of the army.

The wall was still kicking up clouds of dust when they arrived, though it wasn't enough to hinder their vision. Occasionally, an undead soldier came running out of the hole in the wall, but they were quickly dispatched by Goemon.

Chiyome surveyed the city beyond. Since the stench of death permeated everything, it was impossible for her to tell if any undead remained inside. Instead, her eyes were drawn to the outline of a figure standing in the middle of a dust-filled street.

It was a man, dressed in elaborate, priestly robes. He looked to be in his late twenties, and stood around 190 centimeters tall. The muscles rippling beneath his robes made him look more like a soldier than a man of thecloth.

Even from this distance, she could smell the unmistakable stench wafting off of him.

Goemon eyed the man warily and spoke in a low, growling voice. "Undead."

Chiyome nodded.

"Where Augrent and Tismo have failed, I will succeed. I will protect His Holiness! Hyaaahahahaha!" The man's voice boomed in an ominous echo.

His body began to twitch and bulge.

"I am Marcos Invidia Humanitas. I have been granted the title of cardinal by His Holiness the pontiff, and given the task of protecting our holy capital. This is your one and only chance to leave my sight, you and your repulsive comrades. If you don't..."

Marcos's body started puffing and growing, popping the seams of his clothes as he transformed into a hideous monster with tentacles for arms. He stood four meters tall, and was covered in gray-brown flesh.

His head now looked like a pulsating tumor with one massive eye, surrounded by a cluster of smaller eyes. Each one moved independently, making for a rather unsettling sight.

One tentacle stretched across his face in a gross imitation of a mustache, while six more tentacles, three on each side, tore out from his back, giving him a total of eight limbs with which to grab his prey.

The horrendous stench of death emanating from the man, and the enormous power clearly available to him, was enough to convince Goemon and Chiyome to fall back and put some distance between him and themselves.

The rubble beneath the Jinshin clan exploded, and pitch-black stones burst from the earth to spear them. This was clearly the cardinal's work, but Chiyome couldn't tell how he'd done it.

She normally wasn't one to let her emotions show, but this defied explanation. The attack Marcos had used was similar to a special ninjutsu technique that was used exclusively by the Jinshin clan, but it required the user to have made a pact using a pledge spirit crystal.

Goemon furrowed his brow, seemingly thinking the same thing. "Look at his chest."

Chiyome looked closer at the cardinal and saw a familiar sight. "I can't believe we found it all the way out here."

Affixed to Marcos's chest was the distinct diamond shape of the lost pledge spirit crystal, though it no longer held the same ruby luster as the one in her own chest. The crystal had turned a dark black, the color of pitch, and gave off a peculiar glow.

"Begone with you, cretins!" the cardinal screeched. "This land belongs to the Holy Lord Thanatos!"

Black energy shot out of his eight tentacles as he lurched forward, quickly closing the distance between him and the two Jinshin warriors.

BWOOMF! BWOOMF! BWOOMF!

Each shot sounded like a miniature explosion, followed shortly by a shower of bricks as it slammed into a building, missing Chiyome and Goemon by a hairsbreadth.

"Look at his hands."

Chiyome followed Goemon's steely gaze. What she saw brought a scowl to her face.

The skin on the cardinal's massive hands pulsed as it decayed and regenerated over and over.

"Just possessing the spirit crystal is affecting him."

Spotting a possible weakness, Chiyome launched an attack of her own. "Body to water, aqua shuriken!"

She threw the stars at the cardinal as fast as she could generate them. Each found its mark, cutting deep into his undead flesh.

The eyes embedded in the pulsing tumor that served as his head focused on Chiyome, his face contorting with rage.

"Why, you dirty little mongrel!"

Several of the cardinal's tentacles snapped through the air like whips toward Chiyome. The ninja cat girl gracefully dodged them, managing to chop one of the tendrils off as it flew past her.

"Curse you!!!"

Now thoroughly enraged, Marcos stretched out all eight of his hands once again and launched another volley of black energy, followed by a second tendril strike.

BWOOMF! BWOOMF! BWOOMF!

This attack was even more powerful than the last. Chiyome could feel the concussive waves rock her body as an enormous cloud of dust filled the area, obstructing her vision.

Goemon chose to use this to his advantage, moving into the cardinal's blind spot and unleashing an attack from behind while the monster was focused on Chiyome.

"Body to earth, exploding steel fist!"

Goemon pummeled his opponent's back with such speed and power that, with this single strike, he managed to rip two arms right off of Marcos's back. Then he punched another fist right through the cardinal's body.

Burgundy blood oozed from the wound. The cardinal spat out a mouthful of the thick liquid before leaping up to the top of a neighboring building. But the damaged roof gave way, and he fell through.

"Body to water, liquid wolf fang!"

Chiyome summoned two water wolves, sending them after the cardinal as he tried to crawl out from under the mountain of bricks that had landed on him.

"You pathetic little worms are nothing to meeeeeee!"

The cardinal blasted away all of the bricks around him and regained his feet. His eyes took on an ominous cast as a strange energy enveloped him.

Before the water wolves even reached their intended target, their bodies began taking on a gray hue. They stopped in their tracks and turned back toward

Chiyome, baring their fangs before lunging at their own master.

"Whoa, what?!" Chiyome was completely taken by surprise.

She managed to dodge the first one with ease, but couldn't avoid the second. Right as it was about to bury its fangs in her neck...

"Body to earth, tough muscle!"

With a flash, Goemon's entire upper body turned to bronze. He threw himself in the path of the wolf.

"Hyaugh!"

He wrapped his powerful arms around the water creature, squeezing it to his chest until it finally popped, like an overfilled wineskin. Dingy gray liquid poured out onto the ground.

Chiyome delivered a finishing blow to the other wolf, then she paused to catch her breath.

"Thanks, Goemon."

Goemon simply shrugged his shoulders, keeping a careful eye on the cardinal.

"It was nothing. Anyway, we'd best avoid using ranged attacks."

The younger ninja nodded, watching their enemy. When she'd confronted her own water wolf, she'd felt that the ninjutsu magic had been altered by something sinister. There was no sense in letting the cardinal do something like that again. The problem was, the majority of her attacks were ranged, and she didn't have the brute strength of Goemon to use physical attacks.

She glance at her companion. He nodded, as if reading her mind.

The two moved in perfect unison, using cover to approach the cardinal without being seen. The Jinshin clan was well-versed in finding and exploiting blind spots.

Chiyome focused her azure eyes on the enemy and whispered an incantation.

"Body to water, mist blade."

A thin layer of mist surrounded her dagger, then condensed into water and formed a nearly invisible extension from the tip, doubling the length of her blade.

Cardinal Marcos noticed them, and began thrashing about with his six remaining arms in a desperate attempt to keep the two Jinshin warriors at bay. But he was no match for their agility and fighting prowess.

One of his tentacles cracked through the air straight at Chiyome. Her transparent blade caught it mid-swing, severing it.

The battle had reached a deadlock, with neither side able to gain an advantage.

That is, until Ariane showed up.

"Immortal fire, heed my call!"

A spirit magic-fueled flame engulfed the cardinal. Just like with Chiyome's attack, these flames quickly lost their luster before fading away entirely. However, this momentary distraction was all the two Jinshin warriors needed. Before the cardinal even had time to react, they were in front of him.

Chiyome lunged so fast that the light reflecting off her water blade looked like a shooting star. She lopped off four of the cardinal's six remaining tentacles, chopping them into smaller bits as they fell to the earth.

A split second later, Goemon attacked Marcos as well. With most of his arms now gone, the cardinal was able to do little more than stare in horror at the brute looming over him.

"Body to earth, steel claw fang!"

Sharp metal claws jutted from Goemon's fingertips. With a powerful slash, he tore large gashes across the cardinal's face and through several of his eyeballs.

"Gyaaaaaaaaaaaaaaaaaaaaaaaaaaugh!"

Cardinal Marcos let out an ear-piercing scream and stumbled backward in a frantic attempt to escape. However, Ariane had no intention of letting that happen and lopped off his leg, sending him tumbling to the ground.

Flames starting running up the length of her sword. Before long, the entire blade was crackling and burning like a roaring campfire.

"Holy flame, heed my call. Rise up, rain down, and return everything to the dust from whence it came."

Red balls began forming around Ariane as she chanted. They took off into the air like glimmering butterflies, dancing about as if they had minds of their own.

The flaming butterflies fluttered toward the fallen cardinal, surrounding him and forming a large pillar of fire.

An inhuman shriek erupted from within the flaming pillar, then flames and smoke shot high into the air.

Chiyome and Ariane watched the smoke dissipate in the strong wind.

"Think I overdid it?"

Chiyome shook her head. "Not at all. You were a great help, Ariane."

The ninja cat girl glanced up at Ariane only to find the elven woman looking frantically around the capital.

"Hey, have you seen Arc?"

Chiyome perked her cat ears up, listening for any sign of their friend. Alas, she came up empty and could only shake her head.

The Dragon Lords had kicked off the battle between the unified armies and the hordes of undead surrounding Fehrbio Alsus with their most powerful attacks. The infantry had watched in amazement as the Dragon Lords ruthlessly bombarded several hundred thousand undead troops, blowing them away.

While the troops stared, stupefied by the sight, I teleported between the groups and cast Holy Protection to preserve them from the undead giants' death contamination attacks.

Once that was done, the soldiers were free to start their advance.

Even after the Dragon Lords' bombardment, there were still countless undead roaming the battlefield. The elves and Jinshin warriors focused on the man-spiders, while the human soldiers got to work on the infantry.

"Guess we should help 'em out a bit before looking for the pontiff, yeah?"

"Kyii! Kyiiiii!" Ponta mewed excitedly from around my neck, vigorously wagging its long tail.

After affectionately scratching Ponta's ears, I teleported to the largest clump of undead soldiers I could find and unleashed an area-of-effect attack. Then I teleported to another group and did the same.

Attacking beyond the front lines made things a lot

easier, since I didn't need to worry about accidentally killing any of our allies.

If none of them were here, I could've used one of my Paladin abilities, but given just how massive the damage had been back in the Delfrent Kingdom when I'd summoned Archangel Uriel, I decided I couldn't risk it.

Dillan had also taken me aside prior to the battle to remind me that, if the Dragon Lords and I were to wipe out all of the enemy forces, then there'd be nothing left for the soldiers to do.

With that in mind, I figured I should leave the rest of the undead for the army to take care of. Besides, it was about time I focused on finding the pontiff. Setting his crimes asides, on a purely personal level, I felt compelled to talk to the man. After all, he and I had something important in common: we were both wanderers from another world.

I used Bring Whirlwind, a large area-of-effect spell, to blast away a large group of undead standing in my path, then surveyed the battle. Ariane, Chiyome, Goemon, and Fangas were all doing well with their respective forces, and the tide of battle seemed to be shifting in our favor.

I pried my gaze away to look back at the holy capital.

"There's more work to be done out here, but I suppose it's time we enter the capital, huh, buddy?"

"Kyii!" Ponta squeaked up in agreement.

"Dimensional Step!"

I used short-distance teleportation to make small jumps toward the capital before sending myself to the top of the wall that had once protected the city. Though Felfi Visrotte had done a number to the wall, I could still tell that it had once been a formidable sight.

I noted that there were few buildings in the city proper that stood as tall as the wall, which meant I had an unobstructed view of much of the city. In the distance, the Dragon Lords battled with the undead giants.

The giants' black spheres had done a number on the city, destroying buildings and filling the streets with a toxic sludge. It was a sad sight.

Part of me wondered if the pontiff would actually have stayed here while such an intense battle raged around him.

As I watched, the two undead giants combined into one even larger creature renewing its attack on the Dragon Lords with even more fervor. And, once again, the city suffered for it.

And yet, as I focused my gaze on a large tower behind the giant, I couldn't help but notice that this massive landmark had somehow been spared any damage.

"The cathedral..."

The massive church, with several bell towers, was marked with the emblem of the Hilk.

Trusting my gut, I used Dimensional Step to bound from rooftop to rooftop, making my way across the city.

Both Dillan and King Asparuh had pleaded with the Dragon Lords to keep the damage to the holy capital to a minimum, but sadly, it appeared that that had all been for naught. The giant was too powerful for them to effectively fight without giving it all they had.

If Felfi Visrotte stayed on the offensive, however, it seemed likely she'd be able to destroy the giant, though the holy capital would suffer greatly in the process.

The giant was fixated on blasting the two Dragon Lords out of the sky and didn't seem to notice my approach. If I acted now, perhaps I could turn the tide of battle.

Up close, it was evident that the residents of the city had been used to create this monstrous giant. Just looking at the thing was enough to make your skin crawl. Assuming you had skin, of course. What could drive a person to commit such atrocities?

Something the pontiff had said might explain it, but I wasn't willing to venture a proper guess until I had a chance to speak with him, even if we still ended up battling to the death.

Ever since our chance meeting, I'd known where our paths would inevitably lead us.

I clenched my hand into a fist. "Holy Purify!"

I watched as a ball of light wrapped itself around my arm. It tingled, and I could feel a warmth pulsating from within. The light grew and grew as I fed more magic into it.

The spell was used to remove curses, but it could also inflict significant damage to undead and those with an affinity with darkness. It took a long time to build up, and was slow to execute, so it generally wasn't suited for battle. However, it would be perfect against the undead giant standing in front of me.

I used Dimensional Step once again to teleport to an empty space directly in front of the giant and hurled the ball of light directly at its feet.

The ball flashed so bright that it was all I could see for a moment as it grew even more on its way to the target.

The giant's entire body convulsed as the air filled with the wordless, unearthly screams of the dead. The sound was so intense that I could feel the very earth beneath me resonate in sympathy. It was like hearing the voice of hell itself.

Once the light dissipated, I saw that the pillar of dead bodies that had made up the giant's leg was completely gone. Unable to support its immense weight, the undead giant began to topple.

Figuring I could leave the rest up to Felfi Visrotte and Villiers Fim, I used Dimensional Step to reach the cathedral's entrance.

The heavy wooden doors creaked as I stepped into the empty hallway. A moment later, the entire building shook as the undead giant slammed into the ground. I quickly closed the doors behind me to keep the subsequent dust storm out of the solemn building.

Here, in the middle of the church, the thunderous booms outside seemed as if they belonged to a different world entirely. The walls, ceiling, and even windows were covered in beautiful religious imagery, lending a serene feeling to the building.

The well-polished stones beneath my feet gave a satisfying clack that echoed hauntingly off the walls with each step. The place felt completely devoid of life.

"Kyii!" Ponta called for my attention.

Looking ahead, I immediately saw what had caught Ponta's attention. In front of a raised altar, decorative scepter in hand, stood a familiar figure in elegant robes, his face hidden behind a veil.

This was, without a doubt, the man I'd encountered outside the fallen capital of the Delfrent Kingdom.

I immediately stopped walking. It was clear from the way he was looking at me that I'd already been spotted, so I decided to speak.

"Greetings. My name is Arc. I take it that you're the Hilk pontiff and the man behind the recent invasions of your neighboring kingdoms?"

My voice boomed in the empty hallway.

However, the man didn't answer my question.

"Why?" The man's whisper echoed in the vast chamber.

I cocked my head to the side. "Why...what?"

"The way you talk and act! Why did you violate the rules of the game to play that character?! Why?!"

The sudden change in his demeanor caused me to take a step back. A moment later, I found myself facing a powerful magic attack.

"Evil Thorn! Evil Thorn!"

Six ghostly, half-rotted corpses appeared in midair, baring their teeth as they flew toward me.

I drew my Holy Thunder Sword of Caladbolg and brought my Holy Shield of Teutates up as I prepared to meet the attack.

Between chopping some of the specters down and bashing the others with my shield, I was able to make short work of them. It didn't hurt that I'd already dealt with these creatures back in Lione.

However, it soon became clear that the pontiff had only used this spell to buy some time before his next attack. I looked up to see him swinging his scepter again.

Something he'd said a few minutes ago had stuck with me. "What do you mean I violated the rules?"

"I summon you, Serpent Warrior Botis!"

Rather than answering my question, the pontiff pointed his scepter toward the ground and summoned a glowing rune on the floor. A hulking beast with the head of a snake appeared in the center of the rune. It stood at a massive three and a half meters tall and sported two horns, a pair of tusks, and glowing, reptilian eyes. Its armor was made of leather and bronze, and it wielded a massive broad sword.

Honestly, it reminded me a lot of Villiers Fim's humanoid form.

"Jaajaaaaaaaaaaaaaaaaaaaa!"

With an intimidating roar, the serpent warrior swung its massive blade.

SMASH!

The sword slammed into the beautiful floor with an awful crash. Pieces of stone flew in every direction.

I decided it was best to give myself some breathing room. I used Dimensional Step to retreat a ways. But the serpent creature was a lot faster than I would've expected and it quickly closed the gap, swinging its sword in another powerful slash. I met the blow head-on with the Holy Thunder Sword of Caladbolg.

Though it might not be anywhere near as skilled as someone like Glenys, my opponent was able to put a lot of power behind its blows. I admonished myself for not having practiced more and fell back a few steps.

The serpent warrior continued pressing the attack, so I fired off a few magic shots to keep it at bay.

"Fire Beretta! Fire Beretta!"

It was of little use. The creature easily deflected my shots with a swing of its blade before launching another attack.

The serpent's sword was even bigger than my own, so it was pretty much impossible for me to land a blow. I was completely on the defensive.

As if that wasn't bad enough, the pontiff started supplementing his minion's attacks with magical blasts of his own.

With a powerful swing of its blade, the serpent warrior reduced one of the long pews to splinters. I used this opportunity to teleport away.

I teleported again and again, around the large, open hall, making my way toward the pontiff.

CLANG!

I appeared next to him, swinging my sword down, but he stumbled back, barely managing to catch my blade with his scepter.

I knew that he could also teleport short distances, but he seemed to lose his composure when in close quarters, so I pressed the attack.

"Nnnngaaaaah?!"

It was slowly becoming clear that I had the upper hand in terms of brute strength. The pontiff's burning red gaze flickered behind his veil as he struggled to fight back, directing nothing but pure hatred at me.

"Now...let me ask...again! What did you mean by violating the rules? I've done nothing of the sort!"

I continued my attack, bringing the conversation back to what he'd said earlier.

After a moment's pause, he began shouting. "Your strength, dammit! How can a single character take on an entire army?! There's no way the system administrators would ever have balanced it that way! Is this fun for you?"

I let up slightly as the gravity of his words hit me.

In my second of hesitation, the pontiff dove back. Before I could close in again, the serpent warrior stepped between us.

CLAAAAAAAAAAAAAAANG!

A shower of sparks erupted as our swords met, and the whole church seemed to vibrate from the shockwave.

I used my shield to block its next attack and throw it off balance. Leaping backward, I fired off a magical attack to give myself a moment to breathe.

"You're really not gonna make this easy, are you?"

From the way the pontiff was acting, it was clear he believed that we were still in the game world and that he suspected I'd done something underhanded.

But something about what he was saying didn't make sense.

No matter how good the VR might be, no system I was aware of was powerful enough to make you mistake an image for reality. Even the clearest, crispest graphics wouldn't provide all the other sensory input I was receiving. Touch, smell, taste... It was all here.

Sure, it could probably be done in a full-immersion system like you might see in science fiction, but that was all still hypothetical. No such technology actually existed.

At least, not in my time...

My thoughts were interrupted as I felt someone loom over me. Jumping back on instinct alone, I watched as the church pew next to where I'd been standing disintegrated into tiny pieces.

The serpent warrior barreled toward me. I deflected its

attack and then launched my own, using both my sword and magic at the same time.

"Rock Fang!"

The spell tore up more of the beautiful tiles lining the church's floor as fang-shaped stone spires sprang out of the ground at Botis's feet. Unfortunately, it was too fast, and managed to avoid them.

"Kyiii..." Ponta let out a concerned mew.

I scratched my spirit companion's ears. "Don't worry, Ponta. This thing might be annoying, but it's nothing I can't beat."

My mind went back to the thought that had been so rudely interrupted a moment ago.

The future.

If technology that could seamlessly recreate a realistic world existed, and someone were to be lost in that world, would they even realize? Or would they simply think it was all part of the game?

Perhaps the pontiff was the answer to that question?

It was an absurd theory, but it was the only thing that made any sense.

I'd already figured out that there were several other wanderers who'd come to this world before me: Evanjulin, the one who originally created the Great Canada Forest; Hanzo, who'd saved the cat people from the Empire's oppression and brought them together to form the Jinshin clan; and the first king who'd ruled the mountain people down on the southern continent.

They'd all come here long before me, several hundred years ago.

Considering the knowledge, technology, and items they'd left behind, I'd assumed they were from the same period as me.

Evanjulin had come to this world and built the Great Canada Forest about 800 years ago, even though the nation's namesake had only been founded in the latter half of the 1800s in my world.

The only logical answer was that people from my age were sent to the past in this world, while those from the future were sent back to what was my present.

"What proof do you have that this world is a game?"

The pontiff's surprise was evident in his voice. "Proof? Do you even hear yourself? Can't you tell the difference between a game and reality?!"

"Even if this world *is* a game, that doesn't mean you can just do whatever you like!" I shouted. "The residents of this city died at your hands! Don't you see what you've done?!"

The pontiff raised his scepter into the air, as if to silence me. "Evil Thorn!"

I once again used my sword to cut down the ghastly creatures, then fixed the pontiff with a stern glare. The serpent warrior stepped up beside him, sword at the ready.

The pontiff's voice had grown ragged from all the yelling. "I can use magic! I have monsters at my beck and call! What's more..."

He reached up and ripped the veil from his face, revealing the expressionless skull beneath. Within, a red flame flickered. It seemed to be glowing brighter now.

"Look at this face! Does this seem real to you, hmm? This is all the proof I need to know that we're in a world created by the PACC. A virtual world that only exists in our heads."

I watched the pontiff's jaw clack.

I had no idea what this "PACC" thing was, but I could guess that it was some sort of system that blurred the line between reality and fantasy.

I had no idea how many years—decades, even—it would have taken to develop such technology, but it cemented my belief that the man before me was from the future. This left me speechless, as there really was no way for me to know for sure whether this world was real or some sort of virtual creation.

"I've spent so many years in this game that I've become quite bored of it. I just want it to end so I can get back to the real world. I'll overlook your transgressions if you contact the administrators and request that they log me out. There's something wrong with my system, and I haven't been able to do it myself. What a buggy, piece of crap game, am I right?"

He let out a dry chuckle.

"Unfortunately, I don't know of any way for me to log out of this world."

The pontiff's shoulders drooped, but he didn't appear overly disappointed.

"In that case, you leave me one option. Botis!"

The serpent warrior swung its heavy blade down toward me.

KWAAAAANG!

I caught it with my own and managed to knock the serpent warrior back.

But the pontiff wasn't satisfied to merely stand by and watch. While I was distracted, he summoned another minion to the church.

"Hell King Balam!"

A large black shadow appeared behind the pontiff. Runes the color of blood began tracing across its surface. Moments later, a gargantuan skeleton yanked itself out of the shadow. Two enormous, ram-like horns stuck out of a human skull with four eye sockets, behind which was a burning red flame that emanated hatred.

Though the chamber we were in was rather spacious, the sudden appearance of the fifteen-meter-tall Hell King Balam made it feel quite cramped.

Balam lifted his scimitar high into the air, preparing to strike.

"Taking on two of his demons and the pontiff at once is going to be a bit of a problem!"

I couldn't get a good line of sight on anywhere to teleport to, so running away on foot was looking like my best option. Unless...

"Archangel Guardian Raphael!"

I could feel an immense amount of magic drain from my body as a massive rune appeared on the floor below me. The serpent warrior came lunging in with another powerful blow. I barely met it with my shield and was knocked back into the church wall, causing the rune to disappear.

I'd hoped to use a Paladin skill to get rid of Balam in one go, but I wound up wasting a ton of energy with nothing to show for it. The Paladin abilities all took a fair bit of time to activate and weren't well suited for close-quarters battles.

I laughed in spite of myself. Here I was expending magic without actually casting a spell, something that would have been impossible in the game.

"Holy Thunder Sword of Caladbolg!"

Purple electricity ran up my blade as it doubled in length and took on a pale blue glow.

I sidestepped Botis's next attack and swung my sword, cleanly chopping off one of its horns.

"Schaaaaaa!"

The serpent warrior hissed angrily and lunged in for another chance at me. However, right at that exact same moment, Balam came diving down from above, sending me rolling out of the way to escape. I heard a massive crash behind me and looked up to see a cloud of dust and debris. I'd completely lost track of my opponents in the process.

"Yup... This is definitely bad. They're pretty much controlling the fight right now."

I shook my head, hoping to make out something, anything in the thick cloud.

"Evil Thorn!"

"Wyvern Slash!"

As soon as I heard the pontiff cast his spell, I launched my own, chop down the three ghastly figures that came flying out of the dust.

"Flame Viper!"

A snake made of flames circled around me, growing in size as it slithered. I motioned ahead into the dust cloud, and it shot off to find its prey.

"Gyaaaaaaaaaaaaaaaaaaauuushhh!"

As I'd suspected, Botis was hiding just a short distance away and quickly fell victim to the flame viper. The creature's choked screams echoed in the massive chamber as it was slowly burned alive. In a matter of moments, a pile of ash sat where the serpent warrior had stood moments ago.

Before I could congratulate myself on a job well done, I felt a heavy gust of wind blast down on me from above. The next moment, my flame viper was mercilessly chopped in two by a massive scimitar, which also split several of the pillars in the room in the process. Without proper support, the roof began caving in under the weight of the bell tower above.

"I summon you, Serpent Warrior Botis!"

Even as the church began to collapse, I still managed to make out the spell the pontiff had just invoked.

"Wait, what?!"

I frantically looked around, my senses going into overdrive.

I sensed something coming in fast from my left and dove out of the way. A new incarnation of the serpent warrior appeared from the dust, rushing toward where I'd been standing.

While I shot off magical attacks to keep Botis at bay, Balam came flying back in, taking another swing at me with his scimitar. All I could do was launch a Wyvern Slash at him and try to escape.

As I ran, Botis occasionally lunged out of the dense cloud to take another swipe at me before disappearing again. This was getting old fast.

I sighed. I was going to have to do something unthinkable to the beautiful building. It was a shame, really.

I swung my sword and summoned another spell. "Lightning Damper!"

The air in the room grew heavy, and the sky visible through the hole where the bell tower had stood went dark. Lighting began striking the church's roof, smashing the remaining bell towers and sending bricks raining down.

I watched as the roof was obliterated, the smoke and dust whipped away by heavy winds.

However, this didn't actually buy me much time. While it might have solved my immediate problems, there was still the pontiff to deal with, and he could always just summon another one. I didn't even want to think about what I'd have to do if it turned out the pontiff could summon multiple Hell King Balams.

Even if I were to engage him in conversation again, I had a hard time believing he would reconsider his belief that this world wasn't real. From the way he'd spoken earlier, it was clear his mind was made up.

He even had *me* doubting just how real this world was.

I glanced down at my furry companion as I evaded attacks from Botis and Balam.

"Hey, Ponta. Are you able to track him?"

"Kyii? Kyiii!"

Ponta leaped up to my shoulder, staring into the clouds of dust.

"Kyiii! Kyiiiii kyii!"

The cottontail fox unfurled its large tail and started mewing, focusing on a spot in the distance. So, that was where the pontiff was hiding. I took off in the direction Ponta had indicated.

The dust was so thick that teleporting was impossible. Which also meant...

I ducked out of the way of Balam's scimitar, then swung my sword up to block a strike from the serpent warrior. Ahead, I could just see the faint outline of the pontiff through the dust. I briefly let go of my shield, unclasped the waterskin hanging from my belt, and threw it at the pontiff.

"Ponta, use Wind Cutter!"

Ponta cast the spell we'd been practicing together at the mountaintop shrine.

"Kyiiiii!"

The cottontail fox sent out an invisible blade of air.

As soon as it connected with the waterskin, the thin leather tore open in midair, spilling its contents.

The liquid drenched the pontiff's body.

"Water?!"

He reached a tentative hand up to his face. His eyes went wide as his hand touched flesh. His body began to regenerate. A moment later, a black-haired man with a face so ordinary that you'd miss him in a crowd was standing in the flowing robes of the pontiff.

This only lasted for a moment, however.

"Aaaaaaaaaaaaaaaaaaaaaaaaaaaaaaaaaaaaaauuuuuugh!!!"

His face contorted in pure agony as he let loose a bestial scream and crumpled to the floor. He looked at me, pleadingly, with bloodshot eyes.

As I watched, the man's hair turned white and then began falling out in clumps. His skin tightened like dried leather over his face as his eyes and cheeks sunk inward. His voice came out choked and raspy, barely a whisper.

"C-c-c-can I f-f-finally...go h-home...now?"

I scowled as I looked down at the withering man. "Yes, you should be able to log out now."

The pontiff's mummified head slumped forward in a feeble attempt at a nod as his body turned into a mound of shapeless ash. His scepter dropped to the ground with a clank.

A moment later, both the serpent warrior Botis and the skeletal demon Balam disappeared in puffs of smoke.

The liquid I'd thrown at the pontiff was some of the mystical spring water from the base of the Lord Crown.

Since the pontiff and I shared a similar appearance and backstory, I reasoned that his body suffered from the same weakness: the extreme emotional reaction I'd suffered in the hot spring.

The sudden flood of one month's worth of emotions had put a severe burden on me. Judging from what had happened to the pontiff, I couldn't begin to imagine how many years it had been for him.

Since the pontiff had been convinced that the world around us was nothing more than a game, he'd felt no particular attachment to the people who inhabited it. They'd merely been NPCs that he could manipulate for his own ends.

Then again, if he really did believe this was a game, and they were nothing more than NPCs, would he have had such an emotional reaction?

Perhaps the pontiff *had* suspected that this world was more than just a game, but he'd chosen to ignore this inconvenient truth.

The emotions had slowly built up over decades, centuries, until they came crashing down on him like a tsunami.

The burden had been far too much for his mind to bear, and he'd been reduced to ash. I desperately wanted to know more, but sadly, there was no one left to ask.

I shuddered at the thought that, if I wasn't careful, I might become just like the pontiff.

"Kyii?" Ponta looked concerned. It licked my cheek a few times.

I appreciated the effort, but this did little to cheer me up.

"Arc! Are you in here?" a voice called out from behind me.

I glanced over my shoulder and spotted two familiar figures standing in the open doorway to the church—a short figure with two cat ears and a taller one with long, pointed ears.

The dust had settled, and rays of sunshine shone through the hole in the roof, illuminating the vast chamber. Ariane and Chiyome approached me, picking their way through the ruined church.

Ariane seemed aghast at the uncontrolled destruction. She clearly wanted to say something about what I'd done to the building, but I was grateful that she didn't.

Chiyome's ears flittered about attentively, searching for danger.

I couldn't help but wonder how things might've turned out for me in this world if I hadn't met these two. But it'd do me no good to dwell on such things.

I let out a heavy sigh and shook my head. We were together, and we were alive, and that was all that mattered.

I picked the pontiff's scepter up and held it aloft to show my comrades.

"Hey, I killed the pontiff!"

To my surprise, Ariane simply shrugged and stared back at me. This was the outcome she'd expected all along.

Chiyome looked excited as she came in for a closer look. I offered the scepter to her to inspect.

I allowed myself a smile. I'd done some good today. I'd saved people. My presence here, my very existence, meant something, which was more than I could say for my previous life. This world... This was where I belonged. And that was enough for me.

I slid my sword into its sheath and walked over to Ariane.

SKELETON
KNIGHT IN
ANOTHER WORLD

Epilogue

THE GREAT WEST REVLON EMPIRE covered a massive swath of land along the western side of the northern continent.

To the northeast was a beautiful view of the Siana Mountains, at the base of which sat the town of Tisheng. The town had recently fallen to the Holy East Revlon Empire, as a result of their invasion and subsequent border expansion.

Marked by a sharp nose, reddish-brown hair, and a well-fitted military uniform, Domitianus Revlon Valtiafelbe, the young emperor of the Holy East Revlon Empire, sat in a luxurious chair and gazed at a map pinned to the wall. He was in the home of the previous lord of Tisheng, which was, of course, now under the control of the Holy Revlon forces.

A look of unbound desire filled his gray eyes as he stared at a point on the map far beyond the line marking the current border.

A thin, bald man with a pair of glasses resting on his nose entered the room. He stopped to look up at the map for a moment before turning and bowing to the emperor.

"Congratulations on your recent victory, sire. I am Tohd Straus, head of the Runeology Cloister. I understand that this was the first proper battle making use of our employ ring. May I ask how it went?"

Domitianus smiled broadly. "I must admit, the employ ring and its ability to grant control over monsters is quite impressive. I heard you were the man responsible for creating it? I'd like to personally thank you for your efforts. If we had access to even bigger monsters, the West would have already fallen."

Tohd bowed low in the face of such praise from the emperor. "I am unworthy, sire. After I gather a few more frontline reports on the use of the ring, I shall return to the Runeology Cloister to begin work on even larger varieties."

Domitianus seemed satisfied with this response and nodded. However, just as he was about to send the man away, Tohd looked expectantly at the emperor.

Domitianus motioned with his chin. "Is there something more?"

Tohd bowed again. "I've heard a rumor from a close acquaintance that the pontiff of the Holy Hilk Kingdom has been slain."

Domitianus's eyes went wide. "What?! Was there some sort of battle for succession?"

"No, nothing like that. The Holy Hilk Kingdom had invaded three of its neighbors, and one of them, the Nohzan Kingdom, struck back with the help of the Rhoden Kingdom and the elves who live nearby."

Domitianus laughed heartily. "Gwahahahaha! The downfall of the Holy Hilk Kingdom has finally come! I want you to gather as much information about this as you can." The emperor regained his composure and continued. "If this rumor turns out to be true, then that means the churches throughout our lands will lose their influence. We must undermine them as much as possible."

He laughed again to himself and looked back up at the map.

"Soon, very soon, the borders will be redrawn. But we can't let our guard down yet."

A twisted smile played across Domitianus's lips.

Vittelvarlay, capital of the Great West Revlon Empire, sat at the center of its domain, which spanned the entire northwest area of the northern continent.

Exquisite buildings lined the streets as well-dressed residents went about their daily business. The difference between these people and visitors from abroad was like night and day.

A beautiful woman, in an exquisite dress, walked delicately through the thoroughfare that served as the main artery of the capital. Her curvaceous figure drew the gaze of every man who caught sight of her. Her long, platinum-blond hair, flawless skin, and perfectly proportioned face also elicited rapturous sighs from the women she passed.

Amid all this attention, she suddenly stopped in the middle of the street and turned to look at the southern sky.

"Thanatos has failed?"

The woman's name was Elin Luxuria, and she was one of the seven cardinals of the Holy Hilk Kingdom. With a simple shrug, she turned back to the street in front of her and continued walking.

She brushed her hair out of her eyes as a gentle sigh escaped her plump lips.

"I figured something like this would happen when I heard that the Dragon Lord had left. I feel a little bad, considering he gave me this undying body and my eternal beauty, but it wasn't like he ever stood a chance of winning against a Dragon Lord."

Many people watched her as she strode down the city streets, but not one of them had a clue about her true identity.

She graced a few of the onlookers with a seductive smile before fading into the crowds of the busy capital.

Soldiers of various species and nationalities stood shoulder to shoulder in the large courtyard in front of the castle in Saureah, the capital of the Nohzan Kingdom. They waited nervously for the ceremony to begin. Looking out at the crowd, I recognized more than a few of those in attendance.

Up on the center stage were those taking part in the ceremony—the leaders of this ragtag army.

Three of them were human: King Asparuh of the Nohzan Kingdom, Margrave Brahniey of the neighboring Salma Kingdom, and Prince Sekt of the Rhoden Kingdom.

Then there were the other, non-human representatives: Fangas, a dark elf and high elder of the Great Canada

Forest; and Goemon, a mountain person and warrior of the Jinshin clan.

They sat at a long table with several sheets of parchment in front of them. One by one, they signed the documents and passed them on to the next person in line.

Once this was finished, King Asparuh stepped around the table to address everyone. He looked carefully at all the faces assembled before him before speaking in a measured voice.

"Today marks the beginning of a new era. I ask that you all serve as witnesses to the fact that we, fellow humans, elves, and mountain people alike, joined together to overcome a great threat to our nations. We will never forget this!"

He paused between each sentence to emphasize the comradery created here, which defied the boundaries of species or nation.

Tucked away in a corner of the courtyard, I yawned inside my armor. Ponta, sitting atop my helmet, followed suit.

I reached up to scratch its chin.

Ariane scowled at me and jabbed her elbow into my side. "Are you even listening?" she hissed under her breath.

I fought off another yawn and whispered back. "Sorry, Ariane. I'm no good with formal ceremonies like this."

Something changed in Ariane's gaze as she fixed her golden eyes on me. "Hey, Arc...what are you gonna do after all this is over?"

I thought about all the different opportunities on the horizon, though I could only come up with one thing that I really wanted to do.

"Once this is all settled, I just want to head out to the hot spring and relax."

"Kyii!"

Ariane stared back at me, surprised at this reply.

I felt like I'd been in this world for a lifetime, even though I knew it'd only been half a year. There was still so much I wanted to learn, but I didn't feel any need to hurry.

Like I'd done up until now, I figured I'd just explore whatever came my way.

That is, after I got my bath in.

Afterword

THIS IS ENNKI HAKARI, the author of *Skeleton Knight in Another World*. Thank you so much for picking up Volume 8 of this story.

Now that I've finally managed to bring the story of *Skeleton Knight* to a close, I'd like to express my sincerest gratitude to all of you readers out there who have followed along since the beginning.

Though the story has reached its climax, I still felt compelled to leave it a bit open-ended. Honestly, I've always liked stories that felt like they might continue even after they've ended.

Besides, I think I'd like to write an update of sorts at some point. You know, kind of like going back to visit all the places you've been and talk to all the people again after beating an RPG. I've always liked that kind of vibe.

I've passed the idea on to my manager, so who knows, we may see a little bit more of Arc's story. If it does come to fruition, please be sure to pick up a copy.

As always, it's only thanks to the hard work of my editor, the talented illustrator KeG, my proofreader, and all the others who helped out that *Skeleton Knight* was able to return to store shelves for Volume Eight.

That's about it from me for now. If there ever is another volume to our beloved Arc's story, I suppose I'll see you then!

JANUARY 2018 – ENNKI HAKARI

Experience these great light **novel** titles from Seven Seas Entertainment